The mission might be over before it starts...then again.

"Gears, all stop and hold our position." From under his bottom he felt the increased gravity as Gears stopped their forward progress, the gravity compensators struggling against the sudden change in velocity.

"We are holding our position, Captain," Gears confirmed, his voice calmer than Nick felt right now.

Nick's stomach was in knots and the slight taste of bile had risen in the back of his throat. *I'm gonna have ulcers one of these days.*

"We are receiving a visual transmission," said the SIN.

"On screen at my station," said Nick.

The middle of three screens flickered slightly, then the image of Sirenna Albright appeared, dressed in an environmental suit without a helmet. She appeared unhurt, yet her skin appeared sallow, her features drawn and strained. Her normally rosy cheeks were drained of color.

Siren. Thank God.

Blaster Squad #5

Rise of the Empire

By

Russ Crossley

Published by 53rd Street Publishing
Offices in Gibsons, B.C. Canada and Lincoln City
Oregon, U.S.A

Blaster Squad #5

Rise of the Empire

Published by 53rd Street Publishing

Cover art © © Philcold | Dreamstime.com

Cover designed by R. Edgewood
Cover design and layout © 2017 by 53rd Street
Publishing
Print ISBN: 978-1-927621-55-4

53rd Street Publishing
Head office: Gibsons B.C. Canada
www.53rdstreetpublishing.com

This is a work of fiction. Any similarities to persons living or dead are purely coincidental.

Blaster Squad Series

Acknowledgments

Thank you, Arthur C. Clarke, for your inspiring stories. I hope you discovered your threes.

Dedication

For Rita, my one true love and best friend.

Introduction

I really love how this story turned out. I think it's the best in the series but then I'm prejudiced as the author. The series will continue so don't worry about more Blaster Squad stories. I love them as much as you the fans.

Enjoy!
Russ Crossley
Gibsons, B.C.
February 2017

1

ANSS Gallant
Uncharted space
4127.3.4 Galactic

TECHNICIAN FIRST GRADE MUSTY HOBBS rested
on his bottom on the floor of the engineering
compartment, his back pressed against the bulkhead.
His heart beat hard, his breath coming in gasps, and
fear shot up his spine as he struggled to project an
outward appearance of calm so as not to panic his
frightened crewmates. Musty had lost his eyesight
when he'd been exposed to the hard radiation spewing
from the leaking plasma fuel tank, and painful
blisters now covered his face and arms. If he received
immediate treatment, he might survive; but he would
never see again and he knew that.

The bulkhead separated him and the surviving
engine room crew from the explosive power of the
super-heated plasma leaking from the FTL plasma
containment tank on the other side.

The deck shifted beneath him as if it were a bucking bronco and vibrated violently due to the growing intensity of the continuing attack by an unknown enemy fleet comprised of fast, heavily armed ships. The integrity field of the plasma tank wouldn't hold out much longer if the leak grew bigger. Their opportunity to jump to FTL travel was growing shorter with each passing second.

Ozone filled the air, mingling with the charred odor of burned-out circuits and exploded control panels. They had been boarded, and acrid smoke from energy weapon discharges blanketed everything. Fifty-plus dead crewmates, mingled with as many invaders, were sprawled across the deck around them, adding the scent of death to the already toxic air. The air scrubbers were struggling to compensate.

A knot of fear tightened in the pit of his stomach as the ship around them shuddered even more fiercely. It wouldn't be long before the ship would break apart and they'd be sucked into the airless void along with the remaining atmosphere in the dying starship.

In his mind he pictured the enemy ships buzzing about them like maddened hornets, firing their blaster cannons at the *Gallant* and the six other vessels of the Alliance patrol fleet bracketing the fleet admiral's command ship.

When the attack began, the *Gallant's* captain immediately ordered they return fire but not before their sublight engine was irreparably damaged and the nuclear fuel containment tank was ruptured, flooding the engine compartment with deadly radiation.

Normally the entire crew would have died when the radiation spread throughout the ship, except without his captain's knowledge or consent, Musty had rigged the fuel tanks to be ejected in case of just such a rupture. "You always ask for forgiveness later," one of his university professors once told him. Ultimately the captain wasn't likely to complain too much about his modification provided they survived for his court martial.

The battle had been going on for the past hour without any signs of relenting. A deep shudder of the deck plates beneath him shook his thin frame and he covered his head with his arms, wondering if the ceiling of the engineering compartment would finally give way to rain him and the other survivors with irradiated debris.

The captain's anxious voice echoed through the ship-wide comm system. "All crew prepare for engagement of the FTL drive. Secure yourselves in FTL stasis pods within ten minutes."

Musty thought he could feel Stuat'ir, T'Kel, and Simpson looking to him for guidance. He had assumed command of engineering when the chief engineer and her subordinate officers were killed in the initial barrage. Over the past eighteen months since joining this crew, they had taken to calling him Gears as they grew to respect his engineering skills. Even with the loss of his eyesight, he was determined to save the survivors.

The Admiral's flagship, the battlewagon ANSS *Heinlein,* had been the first navy ship ambushed by the enemy after the fleet responded to a distress call from what at first appeared to be a derelict vessel. Musty and the rest of the engineering crew watched the external view screens in abject horror as the pride of the Alliance Navy exploded into micro matter after the enemy targeted its drive plasma chambers. Over two thousand officers and crew died within seconds, right before their eyes.

"How far is it to the nearest still functioning FTL stasis pod bay?" Musty said sharply so the crew would hopefully focus on the task at hand and not their own fear. It certainly helped him.

"Uh, one deck below," T'Kel said in a trembling voice.

"Are the lifts still operating?" No one responded immediately. "Simpson?"

"Yes. Sir…uh, Gears. One is still functioning," she said, her voice barely above a whisper.

Musty gritted his teeth, forcing himself from the floor to stand upright on trembling legs, swallowing a grunt due to the pain emanating from the radiation burns. Beads of perspiration formed on his brow, then trickled down his cheeks. "Stuat'ir, help me to the lift. We don't have much time."

He heard Stuat'ir come up beside him then felt an arm wrap around his waist to support him. Musty extended one arm and threw it across the Xeyrian's broad shoulders.

With pain shooting through his tortured, slight build, he walked with Stuat'ir's help. He heard the snap of their boots on the floor as they made their way across the deck to the lift. Once inside with the doors closed, the smell of smoke and blood lessened slightly. Musty puffed out his cheeks, forcing the dizziness away by shear willpower. He didn't want to pass out. He would have plenty of time for sleep later.

Musty heard the lift doors open, then quickly found himself sitting on what he recognized as the edge of a cushion inside an FTL stasis pod.

"T'Kel, set the controls for the pods and then get in one. By my calculations we're almost out of time." He'd always been adept at mathematics—numbers were his life—so he knew they had forty-five seconds until the Captain engaged the FTL drive. If they weren't in the stasis pods when the ship jumped to light speed, they would be a pile of genetic goo by the time they arrived at the other end of the jump

"Uh, Gears....sir...there are only three pods...." It was Simpson.

Without hesitating for even a millisecond, Musty made a decision. "You three get in the pods. I'll stay behind."

He detected the scent of the Xeyrian's body odor, which had a distinctive menthol tinge, coming from his right. "No, sir. I can't let you do that." Strong hands wrestled him back onto the cushion, then the pod lid slammed shut. Musty screamed and hit the lid as hard as he could with his fists but his strength had diminished due to his injuries, so it had little effect. The suspension gas began to immediately fill the pod and his last thought before he lost consciousness was that the mutinous Xeyrian would lose his job for disobeying orders.

2

Nairobi, African Republic
Earth
Sol System
4152.7.14 Galactic

Nᴵᴄᴋ Jᴜsᴛɪᴄᴇ sᴛʀᴜɢɢʟᴇᴅ ᴀɢᴀɪɴst his instinct to respond to the signal coming from the portable comm unit he'd slipped into the inside pocket of his suit jacket before leaving the apartment.

He smiled weakly into the intelligent, dark chocolate eyes of Elea, the Swahili woman he'd been dating for the past five months, seated across the ebony-colored dining table from him.

The sounds of the busy restaurant—cutlery clicking on fine china, auto-waiters tending unobtrusively to the guests, the guests absorbed in a hum of private conversations—bathed them with sound from all directions. The smells of the chef's creations emanating from the plate of finely crafted appetizers on the table between them penetrated his nostrils and mouth to tease his taste buds.

The creativity and quality of the food here was why they'd been on the reservation wait list for three months.

Special evening interruptus. He sighed to himself. *I should have left the damn comm unit at home.* But he couldn't help himself. Something inside him *needed* to stay available to his crewmates on their very extended leave.

Elea's almond-shaped eyes narrowed and her long, sensual fingers wrapped themselves around the wine glass containing the best Douro wine he had ever tasted, then brought the glass to her lips and took a sip of the dark red, almost black liquid. As the glass retreated, her lips were pursed in the disapproving way they did when he was in trouble with her.

I'm gonna pay for this anyway so I might as well take the call. Nick pulled the comm from his inside jacket pocket and his thumb pressed the activation stud. "Yeah," he said curtly.

It was Gears. "Sorry, Captain, am I interrupting anything?"

"Yes, but tell me what's so important anyway." Elea regarded him with a hard stare and with one dark, perfectly plucked eyebrow arched. "And make it brief."

"I saw Stuat'ir. He's alive."

Nick's heart skipped a beat and his mouth dried. Stuat'ir was dead, at least as Gears told the story about how he lost his birth-issued eyes.

Gears had survived an ambush by an unknown enemy twenty-five years ago when he served in the Alliance Navy after Stuat'ir shoved him into a Faster Than Light jump pod. Since there were only three pods for four survivors, Gears always assumed the Xeyrian had sacrificed himself to save him. But there was no sign of Stuat'ir when Gears awoke from FTL stasis, not even the usual pile of disassembled genetic material on the jump bay floor, so no one knew if he was really dead.

Now it appeared the Xeyrian engineer wasn't dead after all, and the rumors about him being some sort of spy or pirate might actually be true.

"Uh, Elea, I'm really sorry, but I have to take this call." He stood and cast her a pleading look, but her personal shields, fueled by excessive irritation, were set on full your-butt-is-toast mode. Her intense expression and fiery eyes made him think of an ancient proverb: *if looks could melt your face,* or something like that. He could never seem to recall the exact reference.

He headed for the outside of the restaurant, telling Gears to wait a minute.

Once he stepped through the glass doors into the warm night air, his heart was pounding hard as the growing excitement spread from deep in his belly through his well-toned athletic frame.

"Okay, Gears, where did you see him?"

Without hesitation, Gears began to explain. "I was at the transport station in Melbourne waiting to travel to the Armstrong shipyard to check on the status of the *Hunter.*"

Nick smiled to himself. Gears could have made a comm call to the orbital shipyard to check the status, but that wouldn't be Gears' way. Of course, the *Hunter* had been one of a long list of ships scheduled for repair or maintenance for the past twenty months and was still several months down the list before the work would get underway.

Gears continued, his words spilling out like a waterfall into a pond. "Anyway, I waited outside, admiring the ships landing and taking off, when I spotted Stuat'ir exit an arriving orbital shuttle. I watched him enter the terminal, so I followed him inside, where I observed him talking to someone we both know."

Gears paused, making Nick want to scream, but Nick managed to swallow his frustration.

He glanced back inside the restaurant through the glass walls to see Elea receiving the bill for the wine and the appetizers. Time was running out on his relationship with the tall, slender beauty like sand in an hourglass.

"And who might that be?"

"Alliance Council member Anton Kopeck, CEO of Intergalactic Properties. They seemed *very* friendly." Gears paused, then added, "They didn't spot me."

Nick stiffened. This might be the break they'd been waiting for. Rumors had swirled after the decimation of the Alliance fleet that Stuat'ir had been working for the Master, a mysterious figure who they discovered was behind the deadly events of the past few years. The rumors also said the renegade Xeyrian leaked top-secret information about the fleet's defensive and offensive capabilities to the Master's agents before the attack.

Then there were the not so random raids of trading routes to steal ships and cargo and the selling of illegal weapons to primitive cultures to instigate civil war on these worlds like Blaster Squad had stopped on Feros III almost two years ago.

His contacts inside the Alliance Navy told him Alliance Intelligence had received unconfirmed reports of a sizeable fleet being assembled in unaligned space. For what purpose no one knew for sure, but Nick was certain the Master was behind it.

Nick's mentor, and sometimes contract Alliance spy, Asia Call, revealed this so called Master was a member of the Alliance Council and was orchestrating these acts of piracy and murder.

It seemed clear to him that the Master was planning to take over the galaxy. But so far the Alliance Council had refused to believe any enemy was capable of defeating the Alliance Navy, with its fleet of powerful starships.

Have they learned nothing from history? Nick thought glumly. *No empire can survive forever.*

The end game seemed closer than the council knew, and fear had paralyzed the council into inaction; or perhaps the Master was manipulating key members of the council.

Nick realized he needed to get the *Hunter* back in action as soon as possible and prove his suspicions were more than rumor.

He watched Elea exit through the glass doors.

Without a glance in his direction, she headed for the landing field across from the restaurant only to disappear into the darkness just beyond the restaurant's exterior lights. Nick took this as a sign that his destiny lay elsewhere in the galaxy and that Elea was now in his past.

3

Armstrong Shipyard
Earth orbit
Sol system
4152.7.21 Galactic

TWO WEEKS AFTER receiving approval for
the work to commence Nick joined Gears in the
viewing area overlooking the massive repair bay.
Sixteen starships of various sizes and configurations
originating from as many Alliance worlds populated
the repair bays; repair crews dotting their hulls looked
like ants in their environmental pressure suits. The
technicians were busily conducting upgrades and
repairs. After reading the repair projection reports,
Nick also knew there was an army of engineering
technicians inside those ships doing the same.

He'd dropped his coffee cup in the disposal
system before using the materializer to transport to
the shipyard from the station outside Nairobi, but the
earthy taste still wafted over his taste buds, a bitter
reminder of his final view of Elea disappearing into
the night.

Nick pushed away the painful, still-raw memory, instead focusing his attention on the other side of the thick plasti-steel glass wall, where four single-person work tugs guided the *Hunter* into a repair bay farthest from the viewing area. His eyes flitted to Gears, who was paler than normal, his ocular implants focused to their greatest magnification watching his beloved ship being directed into the repair bay. He was shifting his feet and his hands were tightly clenched in fists at his side, the knuckles red as beets.

Nick had been reluctant to accept Alliance Council Chairman Edgar Whizzar's offer to pay for repairs to the *Hunter* after Blaster Squad's last mission. He didn't want to be in debt to anyone this time. He felt dirty and ashamed when he thought of all the death and blood left in their trail whenever they tried to make things right.

The truth was that Nick had considered disbanding Blaster Squad and giving up the mercenary business for good. But now that he knew the name of Alliance Council member Anton Kopeck, who might be involved in the plot to take over the galaxy, he felt the need to once again fight for the galaxy and its myriad of innocent beings. He told Whizzar about the resurfacing of a supposedly dead starship engineer—

but not about the possible connection to Kopeck—who might be the lead they needed to uncover the identity of the Master. They agreed Whizzar would secretly provide the funds for the repair and order the shipyard commander to bring the *Hunter* to the head of the list. The repairs would start in two weeks and be completed within a week with repair crews on twenty-four-hour rotating shifts.

Nick eyed the *Hunter* as the work tugs locked her into the repair bay, secured by thin energy anchors to keep her from drifting. The ship appeared as if she'd been badly beaten, her hull scarred by plasma cannon blasts, and fragments of shredded plating were hanging loosely from the heavily scored hull. There were no running lights or any signs of life. Her fuel tanks had been drained of fuel—plasma for FTL travel and nuclear for sublight travel—before she went into storage. Once the repairs were complete, the fuel tanks would be recharged.

"You okay, Gears?" he asked.

The tech genius turned to face him. "Not really, Captain, but I'll manage." His face sagged. Nick had never been able to read his friend's feelings through the ocular implants as he did with other beings' natural eyes. The eyes were truly the windows to the soul, but in Gears' case, the windows were foggy.

"I really want to be on the repair crew," Gears said with a sigh in his voice.

Nick chuckled gently, offering his friend a soft grin. He rested one hand on the smaller half-human, half-Cygnus V engineer's shoulder. "I know how you feel, old friend, but you and I have the more important task of bringing the squad back together, or these repairs will have been for naught."

The corners of Gears mouth curled up slightly and he nodded.

Nick tensed as his comm signaled he had an incoming call. He pulled the comm unit from his belt and thumbed the activation stud. "Yes?"

"Hello, Nicky." It was his former mentor, Asia Call. He wasn't sure he wanted to talk to her since she helped Sonara escape after the incident on Feros III. Until now he'd managed to avoid contact with her.

"What do you want?" He struggled to keep the anger from his voice. Still, it bubbled up from the pit of his stomach.

"Sorry to bother you, Nick," she began, then paused and he heard her suck in a breath before continuing. "I have a very huge problem." She paused again, then blurted out, "I need your help."

Nick grunted. "That all sounds overly dramatic, even for you."

He crossed his muscular arms over his wide chest. "What's such a big deal you need me?"

"I'd rather not say on an open comm. Let's meet, then I'll tell you everything."

Nick's heart beat a little faster and the knot between his shoulder blades that had been growing since she contacted him tightened even more. He knew he should have cut off the comm unit as soon as he realized it was Asia. He wasn't in a forgiving mood yet, considering she nearly cost his friends their lives and she helped a wanted fugitive escape.

He cleared his throat, the taste of the stale coffee still at the back of his throat. "I'm not sure that'd be a good idea."

"You okay, Nicky?" asked Asia, a hint of concern evident in her tone.

Nick chuckled bitterly. "Don't you worry about me, lady. I'm fine."

Asia dropped her voice to a whisper. "Nicky.... uhhh, sorry, Nick…an Alliance Navy patrol fleet has been reported missing…" Her voice trailed off, the reluctance to reveal more information clear in her tone.

"And what has the Navy's sloppy record of losing starships got to do with me?" He almost believed his own words.

Missing ships had grown to be a disturbing pattern ever since they discovered the Master was behind many of them.

Nick had pulled strings to get the *Hunter* ready for a deep space mission to discover if this connection between an apparently not-so-dead engineer and council member Anton Kopeck were as significant as he suspected. Kopeck and Stuat'ir had disappeared shortly after Gears' sighting.

While this by itself didn't mean much, Nick needed to discover proof of a connection to the Master. For now, all they had was conjecture. Fortunately the chairman was willing to take chance on him and Blaster Squad. Even with the clandestine support of the chairman, he would require as much help as he could get to uncover the truth.

Another missing Navy fleet would be just the thing to kick his investigation into high gear.

The chairman had told him about the missing fleet; he had already dispatched intelligence agents to discover what happened but so far kept the news from the public, hence Nick's mission would be clandestine and off the books. Whizzar didn't need a crisis undermining confidence in the Alliance Council's ability to govern the galaxy.

Nick certainly wasn't going to share his mission details or anything he knew about the missing fleet with Asia, or even that he had already been aware of missing vessels. He wouldn't make the mistake of sharing his information with her again.

"Trust is earned, not given out free like Halloween candy," his grandfather once told him. He had no idea what Halloween was, but candy sounded pretty good to a ten year old boy.

Asia emitted a deep sigh. "Nick, *please* meet me." She was pleading now.

He considered her request for a second, then said, "Okay. Transport to the shipyard. I'll meet you in the cafeteria." He lowered his voice. "And it had better be a very, very good reason if I'm going to help you."

"It is, Nick. Really."

Nick cut the connection. "Stay here," he said to Gears before heading for the lift.

She better not be wasting my time, he thought as he entered the lift car and the doors began to close. *I have a lot to do before leaving Earth orbit.*

4

NICK SWALLOWED THE mouthful of lemon-flavored vitamin water as he watched Asia enter the busy cafeteria, bustling with technicians on breaks or stopping by for a quick drink or a bite to eat before starting their shifts. The hum of conversation echoed around the expansive dining room and the air scrubbers struggled with the myriad odors from cooked meat and steamed vegetables originating on various planets across the Alliance, not just Earth. One floor-to-ceiling wall was comprised of transparent plasti-steel through which diners viewed the blue, white, and green Earth passing slowly hundreds of miles beneath the orbit of the shipyard.

His eyes followed Asia as she walked to the beverage dispenser across the dining room to retrieve a bottle containing an energy drink he was familiar with that he knew contained a lot of stimulant. She appeared haggard and paler than he remembered her. Dark circles stood out starkly against the porcelain white flesh under her coal black eyes.

She wore her familiar, loose fitting, navy-blue one-piece jumper, her white hair tied back in the ponytail she preferred. She looked older than when he'd last seen her and a flash of concern passed through his consciousness until the memory of what she'd done asserted itself, driving away any empathy he might feel for her.

Finally her eyes drifted around the dining room as she searched the faces of the repair techs milling amongst the tables until at last her eyes landed on Nick, seated alone at a circular table. He toasted her with his bottle of water.

The corners of her diminutive mouth curled upward in a weak, mirthless smile, then she started moving through the gaggle of shipyard workers toward him, shifting side to side as needed to navigate to him.

Nick watched her come toward him, wondering once again why he was wasting precious time on her. Why did he need her?

"Hello, Nick," she said in her soft, familiar voice as she arrived at the table.

He nodded toward an empty chair across the table from him. She sat down, placing the bottle on the table as she did, wrapping her hands around it. Nick noticed Asia's thin hands were shaking.

She avoided his gaze for several seconds until finally she managed to look up from the tabletop into his eyes. "Nick, I'm really sorry...I'm sorry about what happened..."

Nick gritted his teeth. "You let the Ferosians die."

When he last saw her, Asia had been appointed as the Alliance representative responsible for helping the beings on Feros III come to terms with their exposure to advanced technology by the Master's agents. When a primitive world became aware of more advanced planets, it created a cultural shockwave in their society and they often needed help to deal with the fear and uncertainty such knowledge created.

Against Nick's and Chairman Whizzar's recommendations, Feros III had been sterilized so it wouldn't become a threat to the major trade routes near the Feros planetary system.

Reports were that Asia made the recommendation to the council and that her position as the onsite representative added significant weight to those on the council in favor of wiping out the indigenous population. Once the Ferosians had been extinguished, the planet became a base of operations for the Alliance Navy to guard the sector and the trade routes from pirates.

She looked away again, hanging her head. "I had no choice."

Nick grimaced. There was little point in hashing all this out again. The truth was that he had asked for this meeting in a public place because he wasn't sure he could stop himself from tearing her apart with his bare hands. "Never mind. Tell me what's so important you couldn't say it over a comm."

"Well, you see…I hired Siren and the Kid to work for me," she finally blurted out.

Nick's heart skipped a beat. *Siren and the Kid work for this sack of crap*? He narrowed his eyes. "To do what?"

"To find Sonara and get her to tell us who on the Alliance Council is the Master."

"So have they?" He folded his arms across his chest.

24

She shook her head, her eyes flitting rapidly side to side as if to avoid him. "They were aboard one of those Alliance Navy ships when the fleet disappeared."

Nick's cheeks grew cold. A knot of anger grew in the pit of his stomach as he glared at Asia. He had to stop himself from leaping over the table and strangling his former mentor. She had placed his friends in danger. He took this very personally.

He cleared his throat, then said, "Okay, you better tell me more…" His words trailed off as the anger boiled up from his stomach. Nick felt the eyes of nearby diners shift in their direction. He realized he had raised his voice.

Asia's eyes were wide, brimming with tears. "Look, Nick, I'm sorry, but they came to me. They said Blaster Squad had been disbanded and they needed a job. I gave them one."

Nick grunted. "Well, whoever told you Blaster Squad disbanded got ahead of themselves." He regarded Asia with one arched eyebrow. "Exactly what was the job you offered them?"

Asia took a sip from the bottle of the blue-colored energy drink.

"And don't tell me it was to find Sonara."

Over the past two years he had come to believe that Asia was working with this Master and that Sonara might also be an agent of this secretive Alliance Council member. Regardless, Nick was going to have great difficulty believing anything Asia told him.

"Nick, the Kid signed on as assistant chief engineer of the *Mars Explorer* light cruiser and Sirenna as its second officer." She shrugged. "There was some resistance from the commanding admiral until I pointed out how much experience they had, and how they'd been instrumental in saving his son, who was a junior officer at the battle with the pirates in the Feros system."

Nick arched an eyebrow. the Kid and Siren were there, but hardly instrumental in the saving of any navy vessels. "You exaggerated?" She gave him a knowing, tight-lipped smile. Nick eased himself backward on his chair seat until he rested against the hard cushion of the chair back. He took a sip from his drink, the bitter lemon coating his tongue.

He scowled at her. "Okay, let's say I believe you. For now. But I still don't trust you." She started to open her mouth to speak. "Don't," he barked sharply, eliciting more stares in their direction. He lowered his voice.

"I want the details about where this fleet disappeared and a copy of the secret sealed orders given to the fleet admiral in charge of the mission."

Asia stared at him, remaining silent. Finally she nodded.

"I'm taking the *Hunter* and going after my people." Nick narrowed his eyes. He was also determined to confirm the identity of the Master if it was the last thing he ever did in this universe. He didn't know where to start looking, but first things first. Get the *Hunter* operational.

As his grandfather used to say, "Once again onto the beach, dear friends."

5

GSS Hunter
Passing the edge of the system
Earth's Solar System
4152.9.30 Galactic

"I'M DETECTING A time/space displacement wave," said the Systems Information Network. Since two of his bridge crew were absent, Nick had assigned long-range sensor scans to the SIN. It may not enjoy a cold beer after its shift with the rest of the humanoid crew, but the artificial intelligence was important to the operation of any starship.

The SIN monitored a ship's systems more efficiently than any humanoid could, and it maintained the ship's course while the vessel was in Faster Than Light travel. While in FTL flight, humanoids had to be in a FTL stasis pod or the time/space displacement wave—that made faster than light travel possible—would cause their cells to break down and quickly turn flesh to a pile of organic pea soup as the cells in their body lost cohesion and separated. It was an ugly and painful death, or so he'd been told at navy flight school.

The one time they'd made an emergency jump to escape destruction, the jump lasted one minute and left him sick for days, so he wasn't willing to test the theory any further.

Even in the stasis pod for the duration of an FTL flight, humanoids were dehydrated and their electrolytes out of balance. *It messes you up*, as he often described the experience to newbies to FTL travel.

Nick asked the SIN to transfer the readings to his screen in the copilot's seat next to Gears, who was seated in the pilot's station as usual. They exchanged a look of concern, then Nick shifted his attention to study the readings on his right screen of the tri-screen arrangement.

An unknown vessel appearing this close to their jump-off point per the coordinates in the missing fleet Admiral's top secret mission briefing that Asia provided seemed more of a coincidence than he would like. Space was a big place and any FTL ship near their flight path was unusual in the extreme.

As he watched his screen, the wave dissipated and a vessel appeared. It looked familiar somehow but he couldn't quite place it.

"SIN, does that ship have its defensive screens on?"

"No, Captain."

"Bones, you copy?" They'd picked up the large, muscular half-Martian weapons expert on Mars, where he was participating in a virtual reality star surfing competition.

When Bones learned that Siren and the Kid were missing, he'd volunteered instantly for the mission even though he was leading in the tournament. Right now he was checking the FTL stasis pods before the jump to make sure they were fully operational.

"Go ahead, Captain," Bones replied in his deep baritone voice.

"Get up to the flight deck to manage the weapons station. We have unexpected company."

"On my way."

Nick turned to look at the pilot's seat. "Gears, registry beacon of our new friend?" Every Alliance ship—both military and civilian—had a registry beacon transmitting a designated code signal so they would be easily identified, especially in a battle zone.

Gears eyebrows rose on his pale forehead and his mouth hung open. "Our mission may be over before it starts. That ship is the *Mars Explorer*."

Nick froze and his heart seemed to skip a beat. His mouth became dry and tasted metallic. How had they found them?

Gears should be able to figure it out once he completed his scans of that ship and its SIN. *Maybe someone has been following our movements all along*, Nick speculated. If that were the case then they might be in trouble and not even know it.

Before Nick could speak, Bones stepped out of the lift onto the flight deck. "What we got, Captain?" He sat down at the weapons station, focusing his attention on the readouts on the three screens in a crescent moon configuration in front of him.

"Life forms?" Nick asked Gears, ignoring Bones' question.

"None."

"What the heck is going on?" asked Bones.

Nick puffed his cheeks and blew out a long breath. "The ship on our screens is the *Mars Explorer*."

"So?"

"It's the navy vessel Siren and the Kid were reported to be aboard when it disappeared."

Bones whistled softly under his breath. "I see what you mean, sir."

"SIN, any readings of stasis pod activity?" He hoped the reason for no life readings was because the crew were in stasis, but he knew, even if they were, sensors would register low levels of life signs, not none at all.

"No, Captain, no life signs are registering."

Nick narrowed his eyes. "Gears, is that ship controlled by its SIN?"

The tech genius nodded. "It would make sense, but someone had to set it on the course for the Earth's system since it's where Alliance headquarters is based. The SIN can operate a starship without humanoid intervention but it doesn't know where to set its course unless it receives instructions to do so. This has long been a safeguard to stop an enemy who might hack into our navigation systems. The SIN is instructed to only respond to commands by designated members of the crew." To illustrate his point, Gears gave Bones a course change that would send the *Hunter* into the Earth's star. Bones shrugged and played along, ordering the SIN to make the course correction exactly as Gears instructed.

"I am unable follow that instruction," the System Information Network responded without hesitation.

Bones laughed nervously, his eyes shifting between them. "What if something happened to you two and I had to pilot the ship myself?"

"Do you know anything about piloting a starship?" asked Gears. Bones shrugged.

"Well, then you better hope for the best, or you may have to press your lips to your own butt and bid adieu."

Bones stared at Gears as a slow burn of anger flowed into his rugged face, reminding Nick of an impending lava flow. "Hey, come on, Gears, that isn't fair."

Gears' ocular implants shifted to Nick and he chuckled. "I knew I'd forgotten to make those system updates."

Bones' features relaxed and he grinned. "You're pulling my ammo belt, aren't ya?"

"Am I?" Gears' narrow features donned an innocent expression while Bones' grin began to fade and the color drained from his normally ruddy complexion. The scar on the left side of his face turned white.

"Okay, you two, stop it right now." He looked at Bones. "Don't worry, Gears will fix it." His eyes flitted to the tech genius. "Right?"

"Aye, aye, sir," Gears said with mock cheeriness.

Nick rolled his eyes and grunted. *Sometimes these guys act like a bunch of school kids.*

"The other vessel has raised defensive screens and is charging their blaster cannon batteries," said the SIN.

"Bones, raise our screens as well and prepare to return fire. But only when I say so. Understood?"

Bones nodded.

"Gears, try again to make contact." Nick mentally kicked himself, knowing he should have done this immediately. It was standard protocol to establish communications as soon as you were in range of another vessel. The SIN on the *Mars Explorer* would know this and react accordingly, hence the screens and weapons.

The *Mars Explorer* reacted immediately, coming to a dead stop in space about two hundred kilometers from their position. Its navigation thrusters kept it stationary. "Gears, all stop and hold our position." From under his bottom he felt the increased gravity as Gears stopped their forward progress, the gravity compensators struggling against the sudden change in velocity.

"We are holding our position, Captain," Gears confirmed, his voice calmer than Nick felt right now.

Nick's stomach was in knots and the slight taste of bile had risen in the back of his throat. *I'm gonna have ulcers one of these days.*

"We are receiving a visual transmission," said the SIN.

"On screen at my station," said Nick.

The middle of three screens flickered slightly, then the image of Sirenna Albright appeared, dressed in an environmental suit without a helmet. She appeared unhurt, yet her skin appeared sallow, her features drawn and strained. Her normally rosy cheeks were drained of color.

Siren. Thank God.

6

GSS Hunter
Beyond the orbit of Pluto
4152.9.30 Galactic

"CAPTAIN," SAID GEARS, breaking the spell of seeing Siren, apparently alive.

Nick tore his eyes away from the screen to look at the tech genius. "Yes, Gears, what is it?"

"The SIN aboard the *Mars Explorer* has received a long range transmission." Gears paused. His ocular implants refocused to quickly scan the incoming data. "Their plasma containment tank is about to breach."

Nick swivel his head to look at Siren on his screen. His heart began to beat rapidly. *No. We've just found her alive.* "SIN," he said, "Use the materializer and get her out of there."

"I cannot comply," said the SIN's calm voice.

"Why not?" his tone was sharp, caused by a flare of anger.

"Two minutes," said Gears.

"There is no life form to lock onto," responded the SIN.

Nick puzzled this out for a couple of seconds. "She's a holographic projection," he said as the realization and disappointment washed over him. It meant Siren might still be dead. He looked at Gears and nodded he was to start them backing away from the hijacked navy ship. The *Hunter* began to slowly back away.

"Will the projection interact with us?" Nick asked no one in particular.

"This is the GSS *Hunter,* who are we speaking with?" Gears spoke to the projection of Siren on his screen. He glanced at Nick and offered him a wry smile. Nick knew he was right; of course there was only one way to know. Ask.

The projection responded immediately. "I am a messenger for Sirenna Albright."

"What is the message?" said Nick before Gears could respond.

"Sirenna Albright says do not travel to Poseidon."

"Gears, what's a Poseidon?"

Gears shrugged. "Forty-five seconds until the tank breaches."

"Siren, are you alive?"

The holo-projection hesitated ever so slightly, then said, "Yes."

Nick could feel the tickles of salty sweat under his flight suit running down his back. Time was up. "Gears! Get us out of here. Full power to the sublight engine."

Without replying, Gears' fingers flew across his control screen and Nick felt the sudden increase in pressure as the gravity increased, pressing him deeper into his cushioned chair. Siren's doppelganger disappeared as the screen went blank.

Gears switched to a rearview external camera that now appeared on their station screens. Where the *Mars Explorer* had been was an expanding cloud of debris, indicating the ship had exploded. Mini-meteors of plasti-steel, hull plating, and exploded, super-heated plasma had fused like a marshmallow held over a campfire to become a rapidly expanding wave of destruction racing toward them. Even with their defense screens on full power, the boiling mass of plasma energy and debris threatened to overwhelm the *Hunter*'s defenses.

"SIN, what is the velocity of that wave…" Nick nodded at the screen.

"At our current rate of speed—it is increasing exponentially—the energy wave will intersect with our position in fifteen minutes," the SIN responded.

"Options? Anyone. You too, SIN," said Nick, his heart beating ever faster as adrenaline poured into his blood stream.

"We could jump to FTL…" suggested Bones.

"SIN?" said Nick.

"Insufficient time," replied the AI.

"Gears, you got anything?"

The tech genius had been concentrating on the screens in the center of the pilot's station and his fingers were busily working the interface icons on the display. "Well, sir, I have a suggestion. It has a small chance of working, but it's better than doing nothing."

Nick sensed his genius friend's rising excitement. It seemed he lived for these moments. One of the things about Gears that always impressed Nick was his creativity and ability to find loopholes in the many for-sure-you're-going-to-die-horribly scenarios Blaster Squad had faced over the years. Nick hoped he had a lot more of these loopholes left in his bag of tricks. He for one would prefer not to be dead.

"Explain," said Nick. "But keep it short," he added, knowing Gears loved to share too many details. Time was too short for the full Gears explanation.

"To sum up, sir, we're going to put the *Hunter* through a full-on stress test to get behind cover before we're pulverized into space dust," Gears said.

"Okay, Gears, let's go. I assume we need to strap in?" said Nick, knowing the dishes in the galley would be a certain casualty. Again.

"You do realize the ship may not survive what I'm planning?"

Nick nodded. *And very probably us with it*, Nick thought grimly as he made sure his seat straps were tight.

Nick gritted his teeth as the *Hunter* turned sharply to the right and the gravity compensators were pushed to their design limit. Finally the *Hunter* leveled off and he was pushed hard against his seat back, his breath coming in gasps, his chest hurting as the pressure of acceleration increased. While there was no up, down, left, or right in space, a sudden change in direction at high speed did increase the g-forces within the ship. It was one of the hazards of artificial gravity.

The deck beneath him bucked under his boots and there was an audible groan as the structural integrity of the ship was put through its paces. *Hold together one more time, old girl*, Nick thought.

Nick managed to see his station screens by turning his head slightly to the right; they were hurtling toward a high intensity defense grid. He knew immediately what Gears was planning. He only hoped the person controlling that grid realized what they were intending to do.

"This is gonna be close," he heard Gears say.

The deck began to tremble even more fiercely and the temperature on the flight deck increased dramatically as the environmental controls struggled to compensate for an increase in temperature on the hull, which was being assaulted by the edge of the blast wave. Nick's eyes brimmed with water, making his vision fuzzy, and he began to cough as choking smoke from burned-out circuits and over-taxed environmental systems filled the air, invading his mouth and nose. Time had run out. They wouldn't last long if this continued.

Abruptly the shaking stopped and the temperature seemed to drop a few degrees; at least he thought he was perspiring less. Nick sucked in a deep breath and blinked to clear his eyes as the air scrubbers started to clear the air of the acrid smoke.

"What's happening?" Nick asked, his voice raw from the smoke.

"We've made it behind the defense grid in time." Gears snorted. "Some of the wave came through with us by the time the grid was reactivated, so I don't imagine the system defense force will be very happy with us."

The comm crackled. "Defense Grid Operations to GSS *Hunter*."

"That'd be them," said Bones, his voice harsh. Some foul-smelling smoke still lingered in the air of the flight deck.

Nick winced. "This is Captain Justice. Go ahead, DG Ops," Nick said into the comm.

"You are to report immediately to Pluto Station," said the Defense Grid comm officer.

Nick glanced at Gears and keyed off his comm. "What kinda shape are we in?"

The tech genius shrugged while he tapped some icons on his screen.

Nick turned on his comm again. "Sorry, DG Ops, there's going to be a slight delay. We've sustained some damage and require some basic repairs. We should be there in…" He looked again at Gears, who held up one hand with his fingers and thumb spread apart. "…five hours?" Gears shook his head. "Uhhh, no, correction. Sorry. I meant five days."

Gears nodded and shrugged again.

There was a short pause, then the Defense Grid Operations comm officer said, "That is unacceptable. We will send a ship to tow you." There was another pause. "The ANSS *Brilliant* will be at your coordinates in two hours. Be prepared for their arrival."

"Roger," Nick said, then cut the comm link and slumped in his chair. "I don't think this mission is going very well."

"What's a Poseidon?" asked Bones.

7

GSS Hunter
Nearing Pluto Station
Defense Grid Regional Operations Center
Orbiting Pluto
4152.9.30 Galactic

P LUTO STATION, ITS external navigation lights
bright in the blackness of space, floated in the center
of Nick's viewer. In the distance, barely visible in
the meager light from Sol, he could see the frozen
charcoal-black, dark orange, and white dwarf
planet Pluto, which gave the station its name. Pluto
provided a rich source of carbon and methane gases
used in the production of fuel for various classes of
Alliance spacecraft and for replenishment of onboard
atmospherics for some of the Alliance races' ships
before they entered the Earth system. Not every race
in the myriad member worlds breathed an oxygen/
nitrogen atmosphere.

The plasti-steel skin of the command module of the orbiting station was blackened and scarred, no doubt due to strikes by the debris that they had inadvertently carried with them as they passed through the defense grid. The intensely powerful grid no doubt vaporized the rest of the destructive wave of superheated energy and deadly debris. Thankfully the station was still rotating, meaning the internal gravity system was still operational.

Visible beside the blackened scar in the station's skin was a misshaped blaster cannon, the twin barrels cracked in several places. At the other end of the station was the crew module that thankfully appeared undamaged.

A tunnel—a rail system transported equipment and personnel between the two modules—connected the donut-shaped crew and command modules at either end. The station's overall length was five kilometers, the modules themselves were each three kilometers wide.

The station was crewed by two hundred technicians and naval officers whose principal job involved monitoring and maintaining the defense grid covering billions of square kilometers of space at the edge of the Earth system to prevent attack or stop rogue comets and meteors from entering the system.

Any ship wishing to enter the system was required to transmit a recognition code before the grid would be deactivated.

Thankfully, the Alliance had built the defense grid five hundred years ago, or the *Hunter* would be so much space junk right now. Gears had transmitted a distress call imbedded with their recognition code only seconds before they shot through the grid.

Nick was more than thankful for whoever was monitoring the sector at the moment they needed help. If the Alliance didn't throw them in jail, he planned to shake that person's hand.

Nick let out the breath he'd been holding. The odor of his own sour perspiration remained in his nostrils and his mouth was dry. He released his vice-like grip on the armrests and flexed his fingers. *That was too close*, he thought, puffing out his cheeks as a sense of relief washed over his tight, muscular frame.

"Gears, scan the station for life readings."

"The command module has taken a strike but the automatic force fields have been activated and, though they are fluctuating slightly, they appear to be holding. The atmosphere is breathable but there is evidence of excessive carbon particles suggesting there was a fire after the strike."

"Never mind the weather report," said Bones from his seat at the weapons station. "How many lifeforms?"

"According to the readings, there are fifty-two lifeforms in the command module and one hundred twenty-five in the crew module." The sensors weren't designed to register lifeforms no longer alive.

An intense wave of anger and horror washed over Nick. If the station was fully staffed, this meant twenty-three beings had been killed to save their lives.

"We're receiving a message, Captain," the SIN said in its robotic voice, breaking Nick's almost overwhelming sense of grief.

"Who is it?" Nick asked.

"Commander Caddowth. Commanding officer of the station," replied the SIN.

Nick knew her as a very serious and professional Alliance naval officer. She was from a planet in the Piepho star system. The commander had risen through the ranks and had accepted this remote posting two months ago when the Admiralty offered her the promotion. She was also very ambitious. And he had been on a few dates with her while on Earth.

"Activate my center screen; I want her to see me when I offer my condolences."

The image on the screen in the center of the copilot's station skipped and was slightly distorted due to damage to the comm system. Slowly the image became clearer until it finally steadied to reveal Caddowth's purplish-colored high cheekbones on her angular face and her shoulder-length, forest-green hair. Her oval, emerald-green eyes brimmed with anger and her ink-black eyebrows were arched. If she were human he'd describe her expression as fierce, except the Piepho had the perpetual look of anger even when they were deliriously happy. What stood out most to him was a swath of black soot across her left cheek and an ugly gash oozing purplish blood on her forehead that made him wince. It had to be a painful wound.

"Hello, Nick," she said, her voice reminiscent of someone pulled from their FTL pod prematurely; she sounded dry as a desert in summer. "Nice to see you." At least the translators were still operational.

"Sorry about crashing the party unannounced," Nick said. "But we wouldn't be talking right now if we hadn't made it through the defense grid ahead of that wave." His eyes drifted to the gash on her forehead. "Sorry about the…" His voice trailed off.

"Thankfully, Nicky, we're mostly okay here," Caddowth said with a slight smirk playing across her purple lips. She turned her head slightly to the left, gazing at something off-screen, then back at him. "We're a little banged up but we've had worse days."

Now that was hard to imagine. In fact, an inkling of doubt crossed Nick's mind. Was she speaking in code, or was it something she wasn't saying? He shook off the feeling. *I must be getting paranoid in my old age.* Then again, nearly being vaporized by a holographic Siren did make one a little on edge.

"We're a little banged up too, Commander. Is it okay if we dock and effect repairs? We're kind of on a rescue mission."

A crooked smile crossed her bruised and battered features. "Okay, Nick, permission granted. My exec will transmit the docking instructions to your SIN so your docking system is programmed for our setup." Every docking system was set up slightly differently due to many variations used by the myriad spacefaring races in Alliance space. "Join me for a cup of Deneb tea when you arrive." The screen went dark.

Nick eased back in his chair and stared at the blank screen. Something wasn't right, but what?

He sighed heavily. Someone really didn't want them to find Bones and Siren.

8

Nick ENTERED THE corridor as soon as the air pressure in the connecting docking coupler equalized with the station's atmosphere and the door cycled open. He pulled up short when he discovered a grim-faced Caddowth bracketed by two heavily armed security officers hefting plasma rifles. The security officers and Commander Caddowth were dressed in battle armor, which had scorch marks Nick recognized as the result of blaster fire; the air smelled of burnt ozone from weapons fire.

Nick raised his hands. "Whoa, Caddowth…what's going on?"

A wry smile crossed her purple lips but her eyes remained hard as two lumps of unrefined coal, with a facial expression that matched.

"I wasn't sure who would walk through that airlock," she said in a husky voice. She nodded to her left, then to her right, and the security officers lowered their weapons, turned, and walked away, their heavy combat boots echoing loudly off the curved walls of the hallway as they headed down the corridor toward the two lift car doors he could see in the distance at the end. The overhead lights lining the ceiling of the hallway flickered, then steadied.

She watched the two security officers until they disappeared behind the lift doors, then turned to face Nick, who still had his hands raised in surrender.

"You can lower your arms, Nick," she said, her voice a low whisper.

"Now please tell me what is going on?" he said, also in a whisper.

"Someone could be listening," she said, her eyes flitting side to side. "Let's go to your ship so we can talk in private."

Nick led the way back through the airlock until they stood in the engine bay. He saw Gears was concentrating on the interface control panel with the help of a mech bot from the station's repair team. The tech genius didn't look in their direction when Nick and Caddowth entered the engine bay through the adjoining pressure door to the airlock.

The airlock door cycled closed with a thump as the seal was established and Nick saw the tension visibly leave Caddowth's lean, toned frame. He could almost smell the fear on her.

"I'm sorry about the security team greeting but we were attacked by an enemy force shortly before your ship appeared at the outer marker to the defense grid," she began to explain.

"You mean the damage to the station isn't the result of our crossing the grid?" Nick said.

Caddowth grunted and shook her head. "No, we've practiced the quick drill countless times. The grid vaporized the energy wave and the debris. In fact, we were monitoring the explosion and your vessel's narrow escape and were ready when the emergency call came in."

Nick stared open-mouthed at her. "Then we had nothing to do with…"

"No, three ships approached us seeking help at around the same time as you encountered the ship coming out of FTL. When the ship that met you exploded, the three armed vessels began attacking us with blaster cannon fire."

"Who were they?"

She smirked. "Well, they weren't transmitting any Alliance recognition codes, so we assumed they were pirates. We've experienced a number of raids lately of our drone mining ships returning from Pluto and Charon with ice ore for processing, so the Alliance Navy assigned us the ANSS *Brilliant* to defend the station and the mines. The *Brilliant* was on a patrol mission and was headed back when these ships appeared." She crossed her arms and scowled. "What didn't make sense was that pirates would know about the location of the Alliance warship when they attacked. Any attack would be a suicide mission with a navy frigate protecting us and the stepped-up security along the defense grid."

"A suicide attack?" Nick said grimly. She nodded and, for the first time since he'd known her, he saw the pain behind her eyes.

"The *Brilliant* managed to arrive in time to destroy two of the enemy ships before the third made it past our station defenses to crash into the command module."

This explained the twenty-three deaths.

"Sorry we don't have Deneb tea. Let's get a cup of coffee instead. I have your favorite brand," Nick said.

She smiled weakly.

They were soon seated at a table in the *Hunter*'s galley, each with a cup of the dark, rich black coffee in a large orange ceramic mug in front of them. The smell of roasted coffee beans filled Nick's senses. He took a sip and tasted the mixture of sweet, bitter, and peanuts with a hint of cinnamon, the trademark of the Piepho coffee bean. Of course they had no cinnamon or peanuts on Piepho II, but the mixture reminded him of those common Earth flavors. Ever since Caddowth introduced him to the blend many years ago, he'd kept a secret stash of the beans on hand for special visitors.

"I'm sorry about your crew," Nick said after swallowing the warm coffee. Caddowth looked away. "Any idea where the enemy ships came from?"

Caddowth's eyes drifted back to look into his. "No. The design was at least a hundred years out of date, possibly more. That's what made us think they were pirates."

"Any life sign readings?"

"Human. Possibly Earthers, but they could have been from any of the colonies and stations throughout the system."

"Why did you wish to speak in private?"

She paused as her eyes dropped to her mug, which was now encircled by her long fingers.

55

Her eyes came up to lock with his. Nick saw a flash of anger flow through them before she spoke. "I suspect someone on my staff was involved."

Nick scowled at her. "Why do you say that?"

"The attack was too coordinated, too perfect for pirates or terrorists. Someone shut down our internal comm systems the moment the attack began." Her jawline tightened.

Nick considered her words before speaking. She was probably right. Her logic made sense. Which meant someone expected these simultaneous attacks to succeed. Not only against the station, but also against the *Hunter*. He shouldn't be sitting here drinking a leisurely cup of coffee.

He tapped the comm button on his flight suit. "Bones, anything on the external sensors?"

There was a momentary pause, then Bones replied. "Clear as a soap bubble, Captain." Caddowth smiled at Bones' reply. Nick shrugged.

This didn't make sense. The enemy knew their odds of success were slim to none. Then it struck him. The no-fail scenario. The one he and Gears developed for the hopeless situations. When all else fails, blow stuff up. "Bones! Scan the external hull of the station. Quickly!"

"Sir," said Bones, his tone dark. Within a few milliseconds he responded. "There's a device attached to the hull that shouldn't be there. It's made of a material the sensors don't recognize. I'd say it's an explosive device except it's not a design I've ever seen, nor has the SIN."

A bomb.

Caddowth and Nick shared a look of surprise the she tapped the comm unit on the sleeve of her uniform and ordered an emergency evacuation.

"Okay, detach us from the station and move us away as quickly as possible."

"Uh, I don't think I can do that, Captain…"

Nick felt a twinge of frustration. "Why not?"

"Gears has taken the engines off-line."

9

GSS Hunter
Orbiting Pluto
4152.9.30 Galactic

THIS TRIP WAS turning from a plain old bad idea
to the worst idea ever. They'd survived the explosion
of the *Mars Explorer,* and now barely survived the
exploding mine attached to the Pluto Station, but the
price in lives lost made Nick not so sure this rescue
mission was worth the cost being racked up.

Gears had managed to power up the deactivated
sublight engine in time to get them out of range of
the explosion that took out the habitat module on the
station, or they'd have been among the dead. Over
one hundred Pluto Station crew died in the explosion
and Nick couldn't help but think, after all that had
happened, that they and the *Hunter* were again the
intended targets. So many needless deaths because
of them being here weighed heavily on his broad
shoulders.

Nick could still taste the coppery blood in his mouth where he'd bitten down on his tongue after they shot from zero velocity to .5 light speed without warning. The gravity compensators had to struggle against the sudden increase in g-forces pushing mind and body to the limits of their endurance. He ran his tongue over the wound and felt the sharp sting. *Amazing how that hurts so much.*

"Sir," said Gears, interrupting his reflection. From the engine room, the tech genius had said he would be joining Caddowth, Nick, and Bones on the flight deck after securing the over-stressed sublight engine to make his in-person report. The tri-screen in the center of the flight deck showed the image of a patchwork Pluto, slowly moving as they orbited the dwarf planet.

Nick detected the scent of machine oil and turned to look in the direction of his approaching pilot. Gears had brought with him the two repair bots from the engine room. Nick sometimes wondered if Gears was happiest in the company of machines, preferring them to people. The bots had built-in antigravity thrusters and hovered over the deck, and they had long, flexible arms so they could deploy any tool or device needed to repair a starship or space station.

Their torsos were constructed of a hardened metal alloy, resistant to most atmospheres, that housed their internal power systems and their guidance and command software. Where the head would be on a humanoid was a rectangular, voice-activated interface and a series of navigation sensors that reminded Nick of side plates. It had no ocular ports since the sensors did essentially the same job as humanoid eyes. Their voice modules could mimic most humanoid and some non-humanoid languages, though they tended to speak in monosyllables. Their total height was a little in excess of a meter.

Nick sighed wearily. "What is it, Gears?"

"When will the *Brilliant* be here?" Gears asked, referring to the Alliance Navy patrol frigate in the sector that had delivered them to the station and headed out for another patrol sector a few hours away. Gears looked tired: his cheeks sagged, his hair was matted and greasy, and his jumpsuit was covered in splotches of grease and stains from perspiration.

"SIN?" said Nick to the System Information Network.

"Five hours. The *Brilliant* is currently conducting rescue operations at the Pluto station," replied the AI.

Nick shifted his attention to Gears. "Gears, how long until repairs are completed?

"We have to get to Poseidon as soon as possible."

Caddowth looked at him clearly perplexed. He offered her a tight smile. "Knowing my second in command she sent me the message knowing I'd come to rescue her," he explained with a grin in his tone. "It's the way Blaster Squad rolls. We love going where we're not welcome."

Gears shrugged then continued. "I still require a few things the *Brilliant* should be able to provide from one of the other outposts, but I can have us ready to install those components so we can be under way about an hour or so after they rendezvous with us."

Nick nodded. "Okay, until the Navy arrives, do your best." He paused and offered his friend a tight smile. "Like you always do."

Gears grunted, one corner of his mouth curled upward slightly. He then turned and walked away toward the lift, followed by the two repair bots. They soon disappeared behind the lift doors.

"What's a Poseidon?" asked Bones from the weapons station.

Nick chuckled grimly. "It's not a what, it's a where. Poseidon is a planet in the Theta Pergonae system. SIN, please explain for our friends."

The System Information Network brought up the image of a startlingly blue planet on the tri-screen on a pedestal in the middle of the flight deck, then began its briefing. "Referred to by its code designation, the planet Poseidon was discovered about three hundred years ago during a routine unmanned survey mission by the Theta Corporation seeking to set up illegal mining operations outside Alliance-controlled space. When the Alliance Council seized the corporation due to their proliferation of many such illegal operations, their survey mission records—with some limited exceptions classified as Galactic national security secrets—became public. Poseidon is a water world twice the diameter of Earth. The land-to-water ratio is two percent land to ninety-eight percent water."

"Any life?" interrupted Bones.

The SIN continued without acknowledging the beefy weapons specialist's question. "The survey probe wasn't programmed to search for lifeforms but did detect a humanoid-made object orbiting the planet. And it discovered the rare mineral fleosue, which is used to power antigravity systems on Alliance starships."

Nick watched Caddowth's brow wrinkle and her eyes flare noticeably.

"The mineral would be quite valuable. Why didn't the Theta Corporation set up mining operations on Poseidon?" she wondered aloud.

"While plentiful, the largest deposits are located at the bottom of deep ocean trenches five hundred kilometers below the surface," explained the SIN in its unemotional voice. "And the probe's signal was interrupted partway through its report. Contact was never reestablished. The probe's transmission took over one hundred years to be received by the Alliance interstellar comm network. By that time, the corporation's operations were under investigation and their mining operations had mostly been suspended so they weren't eager to begin a difficult logistical extraction operation so far from Alliance space while their resources were encumbered by the Alliance legal process."

This caught Nick's attention. He sat up straighter in his seat at the copilot's station. "SIN, exactly how far is this planet from Alliance space?"

The SIN didn't hesitate. "Two hundred light years from the Alliance border as measured from the farthest-most system in that quadrant of Alliance space, the Alagama system."

How did Siren and the Kid get that far out? Nick wondered.

"Estimated travel time to the Theta Pergonae system?" Nick sensed he wasn't going to like the answer.

"Given current engine designs, from our present coordinates, the journey will take approximately sixteen months at maximum FTL speed."

Current engine designs? "SIN, what *aren't* you telling me?"

"That information is classified, Captain," replied the SIN. *Odd.* Nick detected hesitancy in the SIN's tone. It was as if the AI had revealed too much.

A knot of tension formed in the pit of Nick's stomach and the muscles across his shoulders tightened. His friends' lives were at stake and this stream of liquid memory circuits was going to tell him what he needed to know, classified or not, or he'd pull the SIN's plug.

"SIN, you're going to tell me what's going on or—"

"Sir," the SIN cut him off. Something had violated its programming, startling Nick into silence. His eyes flitted to Caddowth, whose mouth hung open, her ink-black eyes reflecting her surprise.

"I must apologize, Captain," said the SIN, "but Second Officer Hobbs is the only Alliance officer aboard this vessel authorized to discuss this topic."

Nick couldn't believe what he was hearing. SINs never cut off a humanoid in midsentence and they never, ever apologized. They had no emotions or empathy about any humanoid concerns or social conventions.

"Well then, SIN," he said finally, "I guess I better talk to Second Officer Hobbs."

"Yes, sir, I concur."

He turned to look at Caddowth, who appeared equal parts perplexed and freaked out by the SIN's responses. Nick tapped the comm button on his chair arm. After clearing his throat, he said, "Gears, would you kindly report to the flight deck."

There was a grunt, then a weary sigh before Gears replied. "Yes, sir. On my way."

Within five minutes Gears was seated in the chair in the pilot's station, looking at Nick. Nick eyed the tech genius, uncertain how to ask; but then it occurred to him he and Musty Hobbs, aka Gears, had a long personal history. They had saved each other's butts too many times for Nick to think his friend was intentionally misleading him. But the SIN said Gears was still an officer in the Alliance Navy, and until this moment he thought Gears had left that life behind long ago. And Gears had been keeping secrets from him.

Nick shifted forward until he was perched on the edge of his chair. His mouth was dry and tasted faintly metallic. "Gears," he began, keeping his voice low, "you and I have been friends for a long time." Gears nodded, his brow wrinkling. It was at times like this Nick wished Gears hadn't lost his eyes. He really needed more information to read his friend's reactions. "The SIN tells me you are still an officer in the Alliance Navy. Is this correct?"

Gears shrugged. "Yes, these days the reserves mostly, but from time to time they call on me for something that requires my expertise." A brief smile passed across his thin lips. "If you think I would tell the brass anything about Blaster Squad operations, you'd be wrong. They call me in to consult about new engines or new weapons or some other technical information to make the navy ships operate more efficiently." He chuckled. "If they take any of my suggestions, I certainly don't know it until after it happens. They never give me credit, that much I know for sure." He rolled his ocular implants in disgust. A slightly uncomfortable sight as far as Nick was concerned.

The knot of tension between Nick's shoulder blades eased. *How could I ever think Gears would betray me*? If it were possible, he would kick himself.

"SIN also says there is a new, highly classified FTL drive that we might be able to use." Of course, he was guessing some of this, but from the color disappearing in Gears cheeks, he touched something sensitive.

"Uhhh…sir…" Gears shifted in his chair as if it had become suddenly very uncomfortable. "Sir, I'm not supposed to talk about top secret projects…" His voice dropped to a whisper as if Alliance Security were listening, which they probably were given how those sneaky creeps bugged every ship in the fleet and every ship that went through the Armstrong shipyard. Not many people knew this fact, but he had friends in low places who told him all about Alliance Security's unsanctioned and unsavory practices.

But given their current situation and that time was very likely a factor in getting Siren and the Kid back in one piece, he really didn't care if the security services knew he was about to breach top-secret information.

He dropped his voice to a whisper and leaned forward to stare directly into Gears' ocular implants. "Gears, someone is trying to stop us from rescuing Siren and the Kid. And that someone has twice tried to kill us. If there is a new FTL drive that will get us to Poseidon sooner, then we have to get hold of it."

He leaned back in his chair until he pressed into the padded seat back as he rested his hands on his thighs.

Nick looked at Caddowth and saw the anger in her dark eyes and the flush of color in her cheeks. *She wants to go with us.* He smiled to himself. *Good, we could use another ally.* He looked at this screen and saw the permission for her to come with them had already been transmitted from command via Chairman Whizzar's office. *That was fast and little too easy though I do love the personal service we get from the chairman.*

Gears sighed heavily. "Okay, Captain. I'll signal the Vestron Station orbiting Ganymede to send us the ship." He eyed Nick who was doubtful. "Since I was lead on the project it gives me certain privileges." He grinned. "And naturally I told them it's a shake down cruise."

Nick smiled at his friend's ingenuity. His ability to defeat any odds never failed to amaze him.

"Ship?" said Bones. "What ship?"

"The X2673G…" Gears smirked. "I wanted to call it the Experimental Star Ship *Lightning in a Bottle*, or the ESS *Lighting Bolt*, but they wouldn't let me name it."

Gears turned away and pressed a series of buttons on his station, then hit the send button on his comm.

"It should be here in forty-five minutes."

"Tell me about this ship," said Nick. He would normally have asked the SIN, but somehow he suspected the AI knew as much about this development as it did about the taste of strawberry ice cream.

Gears avoided looking in Nick's direction as he explained that the ship was a black project—in other words, way, way, *way* off the books—and no one on the Alliance Council would sanction its use or even acknowledge its existence. Gears explained what they were doing now would be construed as treason and one of the few crimes left that, if convicted, resulted in execution. Gears shrugged and a tight smile crossed his thin lips. "That is, if we fail. But even if we do succeed, the council won't admit the X2673G was funded by the Alliance."

Nick grunted. "Come on, Gears, you know me. I'm not after recognition or medals or some crap like that. All I care about is getting Siren and the Kid back. And stuffing it in Asia Call's face."

Bones chuckled, then said, "Gears, this ship of yours got weapons?"

"A single battery of low-powered blaster cannons. It's built for speed, not firepower."

Nick stiffened. "How fast are we talking?"

"Well," said Gears slowly, letting the word draw out. "Tests show it will shorten an eighteen-month FTL flight to about two weeks."

Nick froze and let out a slow breath. "But that's impossible."

Gears shook his head. "As I said, the engine design is new and revolutionary. It increases the efficiency of the standard FTL drive by a factor of at least a hundred."

"That's amazing," said Caddowth, her eyes wide.

"There is, unfortunately, one potential downside," said Gears. He paused to let his words calm the building excitement on the flight deck, then continued. "It will be a one-way trip unless we find plasma fuel at our destination."

Oh, great, thought Nick, *we're going to fly a virtually unarmed, out of gas experimental spacecraft into an unknown, possibly hostile part of the galaxy to a planet we know almost nothing about.* He thought about asking the SIN to calculate the odds of this rescue mission succeeding but it was likely below zero.

Into the breach once again, dear friends. He had no idea what his grandfathers saying meant exactly but it clearly applied to this situation.

They were about to be breach loaded into the fastest blaster cannon in the galaxy and take a journey from which they might not return.

10

ESS Lightning
Approaching the Theta Pergonae system
4152.10.15 Galactic

NICK SWALLOWED THE large mouthful of lemon-flavored electrolyte water and had to stop himself from sighing with pleasure. The trip on the *Lightning* might be fast but it packed a wallop to the passengers' fragile bodies. He had never felt this drained after an FTL jump.

He swiveled his chair to look at the comm station where Caddowth sat drinking from the bottle of avocado peanut butter water. Her eyes smiled at him and he offered her a tight smile in return, then turned away to face the three screens in the copilot's station.

In a moment of weakness, he'd offered a ride-along to Commander Caddowth if she wanted to join them on the rescue mission. She readily accepted; in fact, she didn't even hesitate when he asked her, which worried him, and the too-quick approval by Alliance command added to his list of concerns about her.

She might be a spy for Alliance Security, the Navy, or even the council itself. Or even more troubling, she might be a spy for the Master, the mysterious figure behind the attacks of the last few years.

The Master had an agenda, but what exactly the endgame was, was as yet unknown. Nick strongly suspected he or she wanted to take over the galaxy. The meeting Gears had witnessed between Alliance Council member Anton Kopeck and a supposedly dead Stuat'ir suggested Kopeck was hiding something. Stuat'ir might be just the lead they needed to discover the identity of the Master. He was fairly certain the Master was a member of the council. For now, though, following that lead would have to wait. The rescue of his friends took priority.

"SIN, what are you reading about the system ahead?" Nick asked. He had instructed the System Information Networks be swapped out between the *Hunter* and *Lightning*. He didn't need the frustration of breaking in a new SIN. The one from the *Hunter* could be a pain in the butt, but at least it was his pain in the butt. Nick smiled to himself. A comfortable pain in the butt seemed like an oxymoron.

"There are sixteen planet-sized bodies in the system, four of them within the habitable zone. Two of those worlds have oxygen/nitrogen atmospheres and the conditions to support humanoid life."

"Tell me about the planet Poseidon," said Nick.

"There is no world with that designation."

Nick rolled his eyes. "All right, SIN, tell me about Theta Pergonae IV, also known by its code name Poseidon."

The SIN didn't acknowledge the impatience in his tone. "The planet has a diameter of 24,786 kilometers orbiting an F-class star at 1.4 AU. The composition of the atmosphere is within the acceptable range of breathable gases and will sustain humanoid life without environmental suits. The rotation period is thirty-six hours and the revolution period about the star is equivalent to eighteen months, six days using the Earth's revolution period as the baseline."

"Any signs of life?" asked Caddowth, causing Nick to arch one eyebrow at the naval officer.

"There are approximately seventy trillion lifeforms registering on our sensors. All of it DNA-based life. There are fifty billion lifeforms on the two land masses, the rest reside within the oceans."

Nick took a sip of the sour water, swallowed, then said, "Any signs of *intelligent* life?"

Caddowth's narrow mouth formed a grin and her dark eyes sparkled. She knew he had asked the more relevant question.

"Inconclusive, Captain. The lifeforms register as invertebrates, mammalian, ectothermic, crustacean, and tetrapods. Our sensors are unable to determine intelligence."

Nick chuckled. He knew this, of course, but the good news was at least the lifeforms would be somewhat similar to others he'd seen on planets throughout the galaxy. "Okay, SIN, very good. Are there signs of industrial activity or technology on the planet's surface or in the oceans or in orbit?"

"From this distance, sir, there are indications of large underwater structures beneath the oceans, and the orbital object discovered during the survey mission three hundred years ago is an artificial satellite with two pressurized areas suitable to support humanoid life. The satellite has four banks of laser weapons and six banks of missile launchers. The readings show none of these weapons has the capability of penetrating our defensive screens."

"Are there any structures on the land?" asked Bones after taking the last loud slurp of his apple peach water, then emitting a devastating belch.

Nick looked at Caddowth and shrugged. "He's not house-trained. Sorry," he whispered.

She chuckled in response.

"There is no indication of any humanoid-built structures on the land. The land area is covered in uncultivated vegetation."

"Any lifeforms registering on the orbiting satellite?" asked Caddowth.

"Yes," responded the SIN without hesitation. "There are forty-seven lifeforms on the satellite."

"Do they register as human or alien?" asked Nick.

"Both," replied the SIN. "Twenty-nine human, eight Lobsan, eight Estuian, and two unknown."

Nick crossed his arms over his wide chest and considered this new information. He hadn't expected to find a previously unknown life form on this orbital station. This meant whoever they were, they didn't originate within the Alliance. "SIN, provide more detail regarding the unknowns," said Nick, his words hard in his own ears.

"The scans are inconclusive, Captain, but a comparison of the lifeforms' DNA against the lifeforms on the planet suggests these beings originate on that world."

Nick's heart beat a little faster.

This meant the beings on this world were likely intelligent beings. The stakes now were higher than before. This had just become a first contact mission and he really hated first contact missions. Too much could go wrong.

"Sir," said Gears. Without waiting for Nick to acknowledge him, Gears continued. "I've been scanning the system for plasma compatible with the FTL drive and I discovered hundreds of tanks of plasma fuel within a confined area beneath Poseidon's oceans."

"Tanks? Fuel tanks?" said Bones, disbelief clear in his voice.

"There are hundreds, maybe thousands of starships resting on the seabed," said Gears excitedly. "I'd describe it as a fleet, except it's the most *massive* fleet I have ever seen."

Nick winced. Another of his grandfather's sayings sprang to mind. *When it rains, it pours*. It seemed a little obvious, but certainly fit the circumstances.

11

GEARS HAD ENGAGED the stealth shields before they came within orbiting range of the blue, gold, and green planet in case someone was scanning for an approaching ship. The radiation from the system's star and the numerous gas giants orbiting the star aided them in disguising themselves, making them appear to be a piece of orbital debris rather than a spacecraft to most sensor systems, but he wasn't taking any chances. According to Gears' and the SIN's sensor scans from outside the radiation zone, the orbital station had a very limited sensor capability. SIN classified the alien sensors as equivalent of radar, whatever that was. It was clear the orbiting station was built by a race with a very low level of technology. Oddly none of the ships resting on the sea bottom had their sensors activated.

Nick had a mug of fresh coffee in his right hand from which he took an occasional sip as he studied the SIN's sensor readings. The warm liquid soothed the rising tension he felt after learning of the fleet of unknown starships hidden within Poseidon's oceans. "Gears, any additional specific readings on those ships?"

Gears looked at him from the pilot's station, his brow creased by worry. "Not much more than we already knew. If I'm reading the data correctly, their engines remain off-line but their life support systems are fully operational. The ship designs are varied and some do not correlate with any known Alliance designs, so the sensors may not be registering certain aspects of those vessels."

"SIN," asked Caddowth, "any additional readings on the orbital facility?"

Nick exchanged a look of concern with her. The SIN replied immediately. "By accessing the carbon signature of the materials used to construct the facility, I estimate it to be between five and ten thousand years old. Life forms comprised of nearly identical DNA as those originating on the planet are confined in a tank containing water from the planet's ocean."

Nick's brow wrinkled. "You say nearly identical. How far are they off?"

"Some cells contain elements of human DNA in the life forms on the station. Though most of their cells contain non-human DNA that has more in common with Earth's aquatic life then human."

Caddowth arched an eyebrow. Nick agreed this was an interesting development. It meant the life forms were water breathers, similar to marine life on Earth that extracted oxygen and other gases from ocean water to sustain life. Yet there is human DNA present? Strange.

Nick grunted and stood up, the coffee mug still in his right hand. "SIN, is the environment in the station capable of supporting humanoids?"

"Affirmative, Captain. The air is predominately oxygen and nitrogen and the interior temperature is twenty-two degrees Celsius. The station has an artificial gravity system similar to early Alliance technology."

"Any signs of Siren or the Kid?" Nick asked.

"Negative," replied the SIN.

Nick looked at Gears, who nodded. "We need plasma fuel from one of those ships in the oceans or we're not going home," warned Gears.

After much discussion, they had agreed the orbiting station would be a place to start if they wanted access to the ships under the ocean surface. They didn't know the intentions of the beings on the station, so they had to approach this as a covert mission until they knew more. Someone here had taken their friends and that made Nick cautious.

Nick emitted a heavy sigh. "While I don't know for certain, I suspect they'd recognize us on sight. Do we still have the virtual reality personal projectors?"

Gears' eyes went wide and he grinned sheepishly. "I have something even better. I have personal stealth shields." His brow wrinkled slightly. "They're a prototype I've been working on but they should work just fine."

Nick nodded as he glanced at Caddowth. "How about you and I go over there to reconnoiter the situation?" Her lips pursed and her eyes narrowed, but she nodded her agreement to join him. He grinned. "We need more information to make an informed decision, and we need to find out where Siren and the Kid might be being held. Right now all we have is a bunch of haystacks."

Bones chuckled. "That another one of your grandpa's old-timey sayings, boss?"

A smile formed in one corner of Nick's mouth. "Yeah, Bones." He snorted. "Ya know, you guys are getting to know way too much about me."

Caddowth's eyes appeared worried. "What's a haystack? Do the readings show haystacks on the alien station?"

Nick laughed and her eyes went wide and her cheeks flushed a deeper than normal purple. "Sorry," he said apologetically. "A haystack is an old Earth term referring to a stack of sundried plant matter called hay used to feed farm animals." Her brow wrinkled in confusion so he explained further. "There's an ancient Earth saying involving sewing needles lost in haystacks and how difficult it is to find such a small needle in a haystack…" *I must sound insane.* "Never mind, it's not important, Caddowth. You and I will transport over and learn what we can. Okay?"

"To find a needle in a haystack," she said uncertainly, her eyes flitting between Nick and Bones.

"Exactly right," said Nick before Bones could say anything. He arched at eyebrow at Bones, who offered a weak grin in return. Caddowth was a guest on their ship and an old friend. He didn't want to embarrass her any more than was necessary.

Nick rose from his chair and headed for the lift, his boots slapping the deck plates. The *Lightning* only had three decks compared to the *Hunter*'s six. The materializer was one deck below the flight deck. "Gears, join us in the materializer bay with those stealth projectors. I want to board that station as soon as possible."

Caddowth quickly joined him in the lift as the doors slid open. Gears hurried to join them, getting in just before the doors closed. Nick detected the mild whiff of vanilla coming from Caddowth from where he stood beside her. It was nice and stirred some unwelcome memories in him about their brief romance all those years ago. *I really don't need this right now*, he thought, pushing away the rising recollections of her gentle touch and warm lips.

"Captain, I'm going to the engineering bay to retrieve the stealth projectors. I'll meet you in the materializer bay," said Gears as the doors slid open on the deck containing the FTL life pod bay, the materializer bay, and the crew's quarters.

"Okay, Gears, is there anything special we need to wear?" asked Nick. Gears shook his head but his facial expression was blank—an indicator he was concentrating on something else that was bothering him, not Nick's question.

He grunted as the lift doors closed. Nick hoped whatever was on the tech genius' mind wasn't going to make the mission ahead more difficult than it already would be. If history told him anything, a Blaster Squad mission never went exactly as planned.

Soon Nick and Caddowth had donned matching navy-blue jumpsuits and sound-absorbing boots. They each had a holster strapped around their waists containing a blaster pistol on the right side, three sleeves containing extra power cartridges for the blasters, and a portable scanner in a specially designed holster on the left hip. Nick assumed the stealth shields would be able to hide the scanner, their extra ammunition, and weapons.

Gears entered the bay carrying two triangular objects about the size of a medium-sized orange slice. He came up short when he saw Nick and Caddowth. "Uh, sir, I think I may have been unclear. You can't wear clothes or weapons if the stealth projector is going to work."

Nick's eyes flitted to Caddowth and saw her eyes were wide with horror and her face had again flushed the color of an eggplant. Neither of them had anything to be ashamed of or to be worried about—and truthfully nothing he hadn't seen before—but it would make the mission uncomfortable anyway.

"Gears, is there any way they'll be able to see us?" Nick asked while giving Caddowth a reassuring, tight-lipped smile.

"Not if you're naked," Gears assured him, avoiding eye contact with them. "The stealth projector refracts light and disperses it off bare flesh so you can't be seen. The one downside of this technology is light isn't absorbed by clothing and other objects so they can be seen. Basically you'd be perceived as an empty pair of coveralls." His brow wrinkled. "I've been trying to prefect this tech for the past year so at least you'd able to carry a weapon, but so far everything I try hasn't worked other than the projector itself also is shielded along with the subject, so I am making progress." He looked away. "Sorry, Captain."

"It's okay. Caddowth and I will strip, then you attach the projectors…" His words dropped off. What would he attach them to?

Gears turned his head to look at them, his eyes travelling between them. "The back of the unit has a thin coating of stickum, which adheres to flesh." Nick noted Caddowth raise an eyebrow at the word stickum. The word had been in use as slang for millennia but he doubted her galactic standard teacher was familiar with such archaic slang.

"How do we communicate with each other without being overheard?" asked Caddowth, leaving the odd word on the shelf for now.

Gears' pale forehead creased. "You can't... exactly." He paused. "I better explain. I am implanting a device derived from cloned human flesh into your ear canals. It will muffle communication so that, to those around you, your speech will sound like an insect buzzing. It was designed for use on planetary surfaces, but in a sterile environment like a space station or vessel, the odds of being discovered greatly increase. If you speak quietly using as few words as necessary, you have a reasonable chance of not being detected."

"Very reassuring," said Caddowth sarcastically.

Gears shrugged and his cheeks flushed with color. "It's the best I can do," he said softly.

"Okay, we're still a go," interrupted Nick, hoping to cut the rising tension between Caddowth and the tech genius. Caddowth arched an eyebrow and glared dismissively at Gears, but fortunately neither said anything more.

Soon Gears stood at the control station for the materializer, his eyes focused down to avoid making eye contact with the two naked beings on the transport pad waiting to be transported to the ancient space station. Nick activated the stealth projector affixed to the right side of his chest and felt a brief sensation of disorientation before the room steadied. He glanced where Caddowth had been standing in all her purple-hued splendor seconds before—*not that I noticed*, he lied to himself. They were now invisible to the naked eye. He winced. *Crap. Poor choice of words*, he thought.

"Activate," he said, his words echoing off the walls of the bay. Gears had targeted their arrival for an empty storage area; at least, he hoped it was empty. The scans had been spotty ever since they arrived in orbit due to the interference from the system-wide radiation. Two of the planet's three moons also emitted strong electromagnetic interference that made clear signal transmissions and detailed scans even more difficult. Gears said he'd work on the problem while they were on the station.

Nick was confident the tech genius would fix the problem but it still made him uneasy to be transporting into an unknown environment, unsure what he might find, and especially without clothes or weapons and limited communications. Blaster Squad without the blaster was just squad, and that sounded wrong.

Nick froze when he felt the familiar tingle of the materializer beam enveloping him, then the bay dissolved around him. He became aware of cool metallic deck plating beneath his bare feet as his brain adjusted to his surroundings. The room around them was all shadows and darkness, so it would take several seconds for his eyes to adjust. The air was rife with cooking odors and the smell of warm machine oil. There was a whirr of a fan from somewhere overhead and a gentle breeze from an air circulator common to early life support systems. This confirmed Gears' assertion that the station was very old. Such life support systems hadn't been in use on Alliance ships and stations for at least a thousand years. But he was able to breath, which was a good thing.

Caddowth and he had worked out a simple code word system to communicate with each other and if anyone intercepted their code words it wouldn't make any sense. Love meant we're alone. Shift meant move to the right. Reverse meant move to the left. Ark meant watch out and so on. While they hadn't had a lot of time, they had managed to work out twenty code words before being transported. He blinked to clear his eyesight so he could make out the room around them.

"Love," he whispered.

"Off," Caddowth's hushed voice purred in his ear. Off meant she understood his message.

He froze when he heard the sound of the heavy steel airtight door farthest from where they stood swinging inward. Light flooded in, forcing him to shield his eyes. Rows of light fixtures in the ceiling blinked to life, bathing the room in artificial daylight.

Through his bleary vision he managed to make out the distinctive shape of two Estuians stepping into the room through the open door. Though it was difficult to tell, they were engrossed in what appeared to be a heated discussion given the tone of their words. Without his translator, Nick was still able to make out the odd word. From what he could determine, they were discussing the finer points of the cuisine being served on the station. Neither seemed particularly in favor of the food choices.

The taller of the two male aliens was walking toward them, his boots clunking against the deck plating as he walked. Estuians were bipedal humanoids with skin in various shades of brown. The one walking ahead of his companion had dark brown locks while the shorter companion alien had pale brown, almost gold-colored hair. Both were dressed in one-piece gray jumpsuits and each had a blaster pistol strapped to their waists in holsters.

Each had a small tank of compressed nitrogen strapped to their backs with small tubes that exited the tanks and ran up their shoulders, then across their necks to their pointed chins, finally ending just under the nostrils of their flat noses. The gas slowly seeped out the ends of the supply tubes to provide them the additional nitrogen they required. Their home planet's atmosphere had a greater percentage of nitrogen than Earth's environment.

Thankfully the Estuians didn't seem to have noticed them, lessening the tension in Nick's belly. Gears' prototype stealth shield appeared to be working. And they had left the door to the corridor open after them. "Two," he whispered, meaning follow me, and started across the room giving the two aliens as wide a berth as possible.

Caddowth acknowledged his signal with a soft, "Off."

Nick thought he could hear her footsteps behind him but shrugged it off as an over-active imagination due to the higher than normal stress of the moment.

Soon he was standing in the brightly lit corridor. He suppressed his breathing as much as he was able without passing out and moved quickly to the end of the corridor, where there was another heavy airlock door.

"Boot," he whispered, meaning they were stuck or trapped. They'd agreed this code word should have a double meaning, expecting the meaning would be obvious at the time. Of course, they hadn't considered locked airlock doors that might also be stuck. Or that it would be at the end of a corridor that would amplify every sound, announcing to two Estuians that someone was opening the door. Or that it might also create a trap.

"Two," he heard Caddowth whisper. The latch on the door moved, then the door swung open; the creak of the hinges echoed loudly off the curved walls of the corridor.

There was no way the two Estuians didn't hear this racket, Nick concluded.

Sure enough, he heard footsteps coming from the storeroom and one of the Estuians appeared in the open doorway. His forehead was wrinkled, the emerald-green eyes worried. His eyes narrowed when he saw the open airlock at the opposite end of the corridor. Rather than coming to check out the open door, he instead shrugged and swung the storeroom door closed behind him.

Relief washed over Nick, his shoulders relaxed, and he slowly released the breath he'd been holding in. *So far, so good.*

Obviously whoever they were, they didn't expect anyone to board the station without them knowing. He paused. Or did they know? And if they did, how? A knot formed in the pit of his stomach. They must have sensors…

A four-armed muscular Lobsan appeared carrying a portable scanner in one of its thick hands, a blaster pistol in another, flanked by two humans dressed in purple battle armor, one male, one female, each carrying a blaster rifle.

"Here," growled the Lobsan, pointing at where he stood. The alien warrior and the two humans leveled their weapons at him. Somehow they had penetrated the stealth shields. The mission was over.

"Three. Boot," Nick said, not bothering to whisper to signal Gears to transport them. He hoped Gears had fixed the issue with the electromagnetic interference of the comm and the sensors, or he and Caddowth were about to be vaporized and never be seen again. He had to appreciate the irony of disappearing forever, even if it meant his death.

12

"**D**ON'T MOVE," growled the Lobsan. Its sickly green, hairless face, recessed in a square head as if it had been shoved inward, appeared angry. This race always seemed to be speaking in a growl and always seemed angry, even when they were happy much like the Piepho. Maybe the galaxy was just an angry place? Nick had never met a Lobsan he would describe as soft-spoken.

"Show yourselves," said one of the humans, his dark eyes grim and his jawline set in determination. "You have three seconds to comply."

"Smoke," Nick said, meaning reveal yourself. He released a deep sigh of resignation as he deactivated the stealth shield emitter on his chest.

There was a brief disorientation, after which he looked down to see he was indeed visible once again and was still naked. *One can always hope.*

93

He glanced to his left and saw Caddowth standing near the far wall, a look of fierce anger on her angular features, her purple eyes locked with the human who ordered them to show themselves. She too was naked.

Neither the Lobsan nor the humans seemed to be distracted by, nor seemed to notice, their lack of clothing. The human who had remained silent so far pulled a portable comm off his belt. "Control, this is Simms. We have two prisoners." His eyes narrowed and his lips formed a wry smile. "They are unarmed."

Nick mentally shrugged. *Then again, maybe he did notice something was missing.*

A husky but feminine voice replied, "Bring them to the command center." There was a brief pause, then the voice added, "Alive."

The grin on the man's face sagged slightly. Clearly he was disappointed. "Yes, Centurion."

The Lobsan stepped back, keeping his blaster trained on them, while the two humans flanked them and herded them through the airlock door into what appeared to be sleeping quarters since the walls were lined by rows of steel-framed bunks, one atop the other. Accommodations were rustic compared to Alliance deep-space ships due to space on the station being so limited.

Nick considered making a stand in this narrow room but reconsidered when he felt the business end of a blaster being pressed against his spine. They obviously had already considered the possibility the confines of the room might be a problem.

Nick computed their odds of survival had just gone down considerably. These guys were pros, not amateur guns-for-hire. The question was, who were they and why were they on this alien station orbiting a planet so far from Alliance space?

As they approached the door at the far end of the bunkroom, it swung away to reveal a control room. The walls were lined with ancient computers, and devices he didn't recognize stuck from six half-moon workstations affixed to the walls. Standing in the middle of the room was a tall, slender human woman dressed in head-to-knees black battle armor, her knee-high leather boots gleaming in the subdued lighting. Her high cheekbones were tanned and her eyes were a brilliant sapphire blue, providing sharp contrast to her shiny, shoulder-length black hair. Her lips were pursed and she had her long arms crossed over her chest. She regarded Nick and Caddowth with one arched eyebrow, her features betraying her distaste as they were escorted into the room at blaster point.

The Lobsan swung the door closed behind them with a clang, then locked it. The command center smelled of electrical discharge and burned-out circuits. Not surprising given how long this facility had been orbiting this world. Nick wondered how the orbit had remained stable all these millennia. *Amazing the small stuff I think about when I'm about to be vaporized,* he mused.

Looking around, Nick saw there were six additional guards, all armed with blaster rifles, standing in the shadows near the corners of the command center, ready for any aggressive move Caddowth or he might make. He wondered where the rest of the crew might be.

"Have you interrogated them?" the woman barked at the guard who brought them, her eyes flaring with inner fury.

Why hadn't Gears transported them yet?

"No, Centurion, I haven't…not yet…" said the man who had identified himself earlier as Simms. His voice trailed off, fear underpinning his words.

The woman abruptly dropped her arms to her sides, then approached Simms. Nick saw him begin to tremble and involuntarily suck in a breath. His eyes were wide and a few beads of perspiration appeared on his forehead.

He looks like he's freaking out, thought Nick. He studied the woman as she approached Simms, her eyes narrowing, her lips forming a sneer. It was then Nick noticed the sheath containing a knife on her hip. As she came closer to Simms, she pulled the knife from the sheath, the polished blade glinting as it caught the light. With one swift, fluid movement, she raised the blade and swung it sideways across Simms' throat, then stepped to one side.

She must have severed the carotid artery because blood spurted across the deck from the wound. Nick and Caddowth were forced to move back so as not to step in the warm liquid quickly growing to an expanding pool of dark red. Simms' hand released his blaster and it clattered to the deck. Then his hands moved to his throat, desperately trying to stem the flow as his fearful eyes looked to his comrades for assistance. He sank to his knees, struggling but failing to speak. A gasp quickly swallowed by a gurgle came out of his shredded throat as his eyes rolled up. He collapsed face down on the deck into a pool of his blood. Simms' body sagged like a balloon with a leak. Finally he shuddered twice before emitting a final death rattle and ceased moving.

The woman snorted derisively, an arrogant half smile on her lips as she bent forward and wiped Simms' blood off the knife blade onto his uniform before sheathing it once again. Her features became hard again, and as she stood upright, her intense eyes shifted between the remaining guards. "Throw this out with the garbage," she said.

"Yes, Centurion," replied the muscular Lobsan, who moved quickly to pick up Simms' limp corpse and throw it across his left shoulder. He glanced over his opposite shoulder at the other human guard. "Get someone to clean the deck," the large four-armed alien ordered. The human nodded, his eyes still registering surprise at what had just occurred.

Nick glanced at Caddowth, whose purple cheeks were pale. He looked back to lock eyes with the Centurion. "Is this what you have in store for us?" he asked.

The woman chuckled grimly. "No. Once you have told us what we want to know, you two are going out an airlock. I wouldn't want to stain my favorite knife with your blood.

"Guards," said the Centurion, her eyes shifting to one of the guards in shadows. "Take them to the lab." She looked back at Nick, a sinister smile on her lips. "There's something I need you to see."

The guards came up beside them and urged them, with the business end of their blaster rifles, to walk ahead of two of them. They soon came to another closed steel door. It swung aside to reveal a brightly lit room swarming with humans and aliens surrounding two steel coffin-like tanks resting on stands in the middle of the room.

As they entered the room, Nick noted there were portable machines connected to the tanks. He assumed one had to be a water circulator since, when he came up beside the tank, he saw there was a window on the top through which he could see water. An alien was inside that made his heart skip a beat. The face looked like Siren's but the flesh was a light blue and covered with what appeared to be fish scales. The eyes were closed. Her luxurious hair was missing and there appeared to be gills on both sides of the neck.

He glanced at the other tank and saw the Kid in the same condition as Siren. The one difference was his eyes were open and looking at him pleadingly. Nick walked to stand over the tank containing the Kid. The young man's appearance had been radically transformed into a hybrid between a sea creature and a humanoid. The Kid peered back at him, his eyes fearful.

Nick's heart pounded and his mouth was dry. What had happened here?

"Kid," he said leaning closer. "Can you hear me?"

The Kid's black eyes blinked and he nodded sharply. Sound carried in water. His words would sound muffled but at least the younger man, or whatever he was now, would be able to understand him.

"He's upsetting the specimen," said a high-pitched male voice.

Nick shifted his gaze to his left and saw a short, rotund man with a ring of carrot-colored hair surrounding a baldhead. He had his hands buried in the pockets of a white lab coat buttoned up to almost his neckline. His pale green, watery eyes were fixed on Nick and a wry smile formed on his pale lips.

The burn of anger rose from Nick's belly to deposit the taste of sour bile at the back of his throat. "Who are you?" he said between gritted teeth.

Two guards approached Nick from the left and the right, then grabbed him by the shoulders. With one sharp jerk, they simultaneously pulled him roughly away from the tank containing the Kid. As if on cue, the woman who was called Centurion appeared on the opposite side of the tanks, her eyes watchful as she regarded them.

Nick glanced over his shoulder and glared daggers at one of the grim-faced guards, his eyes flicking briefly to the blaster rifle in the guard's other hand, the butt resting on his hip, the barrel pointed at the ceiling. Nick considered how he would elbow the guard in the gut, grab the rifle, and shoot the woman before the other guard cut him down.

"What's going on here?" the woman said, her tone threatening.

The man in the lab coat grunted and emitted a sharp bark of a laugh. "Your guests are trying to interfere with our specimens." The centurion's eyes narrowed. "But of course I'm not about to let that happen."

The centurion shook her head. She walked to one end of the tanks and stood staring at Nick, then shifting her steady, confident gaze to Caddowth. "As you can see, Captain Justice, we have made modifications to your former crewmates." She cocked her head slightly to the left, a gesture reminding Nick of his dog Otis Redding he'd had when he was a kid. "Aren't you the least bit curious why?"

Nick forced the tension from between his shoulder blades and had to restrain himself from glancing at the blaster rifle being held by the guard to his right.

It'd be better to be dead than turned into a half fish man or whatever had been done to his friends. *How does she know who I am*? He offered her a tight smile.

"Naturally…" He began a countdown in his head: *Five…four…three…two…noooo…* He stopped counting when the familiar tingling of a materializer beam enveloped his body, freezing him where he stood. The lab, the guards, the tanks, and the surprised expression of the centurion began to fade from view.

13

ESS Lightning
Orbiting Theta Pergonae IV aka Poseidon
4152.10.19 Galactic

"Gears!" Nick shouted as soon as the materializer beam released him. He was breathing hard and trembling with anger.

"Sir?" said a clearly puzzled Gears, standing at the control console of the materializer. His ocular implants whirred as they adjusted to focus on Nick's face.

Beside Nick, Caddowth placed one hand on his arm, then pulled it back sharply as if she'd touched a flame when he turned to glare at her. "Don't worry, Nicky, we'll get them back."

"What happened over there?" asked Bones, who stood in the open bay door. He scanned Caddowth and Nick up and down. "You two seem okay."

"Well, we're *not* okay," said Nick, burying his face in his hands. *How could I have been so stupid?*

Asia must have known where she was sending Siren and the Kid, and she must have at least heard of the technology they'd used to transform his friends. She wanted that tech. And she wanted them to steal it.

Asia sent him on this rescue mission to confirm the technology was real, and if they didn't succeed, she'd send in some other mercenary team to retrieve it. And now they had confirmed it was real. His eyes narrowed and shifted his gaze to look at Caddowth.

"You're working for Asia, aren't you?" Nick said between gritted teeth. He raised his head from between his hands, and his fingers curled to form fists as he dropped his arms to his sides.

Caddowth avoided his eyes by looking away at a blank wall of the bay. By her reaction, it confirmed she was reporting their movements to Asia. But she wasn't going to tell his old mentor about this new development. At least not yet.

"Bones," he said slowly, "give her some clothes, then lock her in the brig."

"We don't have a brig," replied Bones.

Nick snorted, then looked at his large, muscular friend with a lopsided grin on his lips. "Then lock her in a cabin. And make sure she doesn't have access to the comm, or anything she might use to signal anyone."

He looked at Caddowth, who was still avoiding looking at him.

Bones approached the transport pad and grabbed her by one arm. She winced but didn't struggle, not that it would have done any good. Due to being born and raised on Mars, Bones had the strength of three Earth-born humans. "Come on," he said gruffly, abandoning her navy designation as a commander. With Caddowth in tow, Bones disappeared into the lift.

Nick stepped off the transport pad. "Get me some clothes," he said as the stress and tension dropped away leaving him exhausted. He could have used a nap right now but there was still much to do if he was going to retrieve his friends and steal the alien technology to transform his friends back to fully human. If it was possible at all. Gears appeared at his side with his flight suit, boots, and a blaster pistol in a holster. He set them on the edge of the platform next to Nick.

"Thank you, old friend," he whispered.

Gears' brow wrinkled. "So tell me, Captain, what did you see over there?"

Nick sighed as he began to dress, the smell of the freshly polished leather boots filling his nostrils. It felt good to have clothes on again.

"I found Siren and the Kid aboard the station."

"So what's the problem? I'll transport them out of there."

Nick shook his head as he grasped the flight suit's zipper and pulled it up. "No, we can't. They've been transformed. If we try to transport them without making special arrangements, they will die." He looked at Gears. "We don't have the facilities."

"Transformed? Into what?"

"They're been changed into some form of hybrid between humans and sea life." Gears opened his mouth to speak but Nick held up one hand to stop him. "Before you ask, I don't know how or why or who's responsible." He shifted his gaze to the deck. "I have some suspects." He stood straight and clipped his holster into place, taking time to adjust the weight of the pistol so it hung where he could easily pull it if he needed to.

"Like who, sir?" Gears asked. His voice sounded deeper, threatening. Nick knew when the normally soft-spoken tech genius, who loved kittens and puppies, was angered, he was deadly with all sorts of weaponry from throwing knives to blaster cannons and everything in between. He'd seen the engineer in action and vowed, then, never to get on his bad side.

"Walk with me," Nick said as he turned and walked to the lift.

Once in the lift car and headed for the command deck, he said, "I met a human woman on that station who the guards referred to as Centurion, and also a human man who said Siren and the Kid were specimens. I think this means he was the one responsible for their transformation." Nick had decided to refer to the man as a scientist based on his wearing a lab coat, though he might not be. He might be something else.

"So what's our next move?"

The doors opened and they exited onto the flight deck. "We take that station and capture that scientist." He glanced at Gears, walking beside him, as they approached the pilot and copilot stations. "And we steal whatever device or technology they used to make the transformation."

Bones was already at the weapons station running diagnostics. "You're talking music to my hearing," he said with a grim smile.

Nick thought about correcting Bones' butchering of an ancient saying but instead chuckled. "You're absolutely on target, Bones."

14

ESS Lightning
Orbiting Theta Pergonae IV aka Poseidon
4152.10.19 Galactic

GEARS STOOD AT the controls of the materializer, about to transport Bones, Nick, and himself onto the alien space station. The SIN would maintain the vessel's position until they transmitted the recall code.

They were dressed in armored battle suits and each had a blaster rifle and two pistols, one on each hip in holsters. Each of them also carried three concussion grenades designed to disable, not kill, and a razor sharp battle knife kept in a sheath next to the pistol on their right side. Nick had also slipped an implosion grenade onto his belt as insurance. Additionally Gears had a portable scanner affixed to his belt by a magnetic clip.

"Okay, SIN," Gears said after setting the target coordinates. His husky voice echoed from inside his helmet.

"When I give you the signal, transport us aboard that station, then take the ship to orbit the closest of the three moons and wait for the retrieval code."

"Yes, sir," replied the artificial intelligence in its machine voice over his suit comm.

Nick was worried the ship's shielding had been penetrated by unknown means. It seemed unlikely since so far there hadn't been any indication they'd been discovered, but he wasn't taking any chances with their ride home.

He fully expected they'd be detected this time. The plan was to transport into the laboratory and take out any opposition. Block any entrances or exits after securing the water tanks holding their friends, the scientist, and the alien tech that made the transformation possible. They would then send the retrieval signal in a narrow beam, high-speed signal to the *Lighting* and hopefully they and the tanks holding their friends would be transported back without incurring casualties while inflicting a few in the process. Nick smiled to himself. *Is that all?*

They moved into a triangular defensive pattern, their backs to each other. Nick raised the rifle in case he needed to fire the moment they materialized on the station.

He heard the others do the same, followed by the muffled clicks of the safety switches being disengaged. His heart beat hard, he could hear his own breathing inside his helmet, and his mouth tasted metallic. Being sent into a hostile environment had always heightened his senses since his first day of basic training. He'd always managed to do his job as well if not better than his fellow recruits in those days, but the initial feelings of uncertainty before a battle had never left him. Maybe it was what kept him alive through the too-terrible-to-talk-about times during his service in the Alliance Navy all those years ago. He had never regretted leaving the Navy to start Blaster Squad, not once, until today.

Today his closest friends in the galaxy might die because of his ego and his compulsion to show Asia she was wrong to send him to stop whatever her latest deception was really about.

She must want this alien technology very badly, and he would deny her even if it meant she placed a bounty on his head, which Asia would probably do as soon as she learned what he and the squad had done. Of course, bounties would also be placed on his team's heads to intimidate him, and it would work.

Nick had always placed his team's lives ahead of his own and Asia knew this.

They would never know what he was willing to sacrifice for them.

His thoughts were interrupted when he heard Gears utter the signal. The tingling began deep in his gut and quickly spread throughout his body and the *Lightning*'s materializer bay became hazy until it finally disappeared.

When he next became aware of his surroundings, he found himself pointing his blaster rifle at the red-haired scientist, who looked as pale as a freshly washed bed sheet. His eyes were wide with fear.

"No one move," barked Bones, sweeping his rifle from left to right, then back again. "No one has to die today unless they feel the need to." His dark eyes narrowed.

Nick scanned around the room and saw there were two guards and the scientist. No containment tanks holding his friends. No centurion. And the lab appeared to have been stripped of the equipment he'd seen when he was last here.

Bones moved to his right, keeping his rifle trained on the two guards. "Drop your weapons." He wore a deep scowl on his rugged features, accompanied by a glaring intensity in his eyes that often scared even the most battle-hardened enemy into submission.

The guards immediately dropped their rifles and their blaster pistols to the deck, the weapons landing with a loud clang, and raised their hands in surrender. "Now lie face down, your hands locked behind your heads," ordered Bones. Again the two guards complied without uttering a word of protest.

Nick shook his head and grunted, keeping his attention focused on the sweating, trembling scientist. He must have never been in a battle or faced anyone pointing a gun at him before to be this scared. "Where are the tanks?" Nick asked the man, stepping closer to him.

"Uhhhh...they're gone."

Nick snorted in disgust. "I know that, but where?"

"Uhhh...they've been transported to the planet."

"Gears, scan the station." Nick arched an eyebrow and eyed the scientist. "He's probably lying." He took another step forward, causing the scientist to step back. "What's your name, scientist?"

"Uhhh...I'm not a scientist. I'm an engineer...a genetic engineer...uhhh...my name's Sheldon, Sidney Sheldon."

"How did you do it?" Nick said.

"Do what?"

"If you keep being evasive, I'm going to rearrange your body so that your arms are where your legs are now, and vice versa." He leveled his blaster rifle at Sidney's face.

"Please…no…I'll tell you whatever you want to know. Just *please* don't kill me."

Nick's eyes narrowed. "Oh, don't worry, Sheldon, I'm not going to kill you. I'm going to do much, much worse things than kill you." He wanted to burst out laughing at his inane words but managed to restrain himself. Good thing, too, since Sidney Sheldon's increased shaking-in-his-boots, bladder-about-to-give-way look of wide-eyed fear meant this nonsensical language was working.

The truth was, Nick had never killed anyone in cold blood nor would he ever. But Sidney didn't have to know that he had personal boundaries. Even if this guy had transformed his friends into hybrid creatures, Nick wouldn't kill him. He'd take him back to face Alliance justice for his crimes. They might execute him, but Nick wouldn't be responsible. Genetic engineering was illegal in the Alliance and had been for two thousand years. This meant old Sidney here wasn't from the Alliance, so where was he from and how did he end up here? More importantly, who was he working for?

Nick arched one brow and lowered the rifle barrel. "Okay. Tell me everything once we get back to our ship."

"Gears, anything?"

"Nope, sorry, Captain, but we, these two guards," he nodded at the two men lying on their stomachs on the deck, "and Sidney here, are the only beings aboard this station. As far as I can tell from the residual background radiation, everyone and all their equipment have been transported to the planet. Possibly onto one of those ships we discovered on the seabed."

"Okay. I'm transmitting the retrieval code now," Nick said. He pressed the button on his comm that would transmit code black27 to the *Lightning*. The SIN would bring the ship into orbit within ten minutes. He shifted his gaze to stare at Sidney. Something seemed oddly familiar about him. *Perhaps someone described him to me*? But who and when?

"Sidney, sit on the deck and lower your hands. We need to have a little talk before we're transported to my ship." Sidney sat cross-legged on the deck, his hands buried in his lap. His droopy, watery eyes reminded Nick of a puppy he once owned.

Nick slung his rifle over his back and leaned closer to the frightened genetic engineer to study the man's eyes. "Do we know each other?"

Sidney shrugged. "Maybe," he said, avoiding Nick's gaze.

Nick stood upright. "Gears, scan this guy, will ya. I think he's not who he appears to be."

Sidney's uncertain gaze shifted to Gears, who held up the portable scanner. The tech genius read the readout screen as his brow creased deeper and deeper. "Captain, what we have here is a man wearing a disguise."

Nick looked Sidney up and down, trying to determine how he could be wearing a disguise. "I don't see it, Gears. He looks...I don't know... normal?"

"Sorry, I was being inexact again. This person has been genetically altered to look like the man we see before us. He didn't look this way before his genetic structure was transformed."

Nick's cheeks grew cool. "So who exactly are we looking at?"

Gears puffed his cheeks out and shook his head. "Well, if my readings are accurate, and I'm reasonably sure they are because I checked them with the SIN, this man is Stuat'ir."

15

"S<small>TUAT'IR</small>?"

Gears nodded.

Nick eyed the shaking, trembling man seated before him. He could smell the fear on him. He reeked of fried Kuptul snake sweat. "Did the SIN confirm his DNA scans against the navy records?"

"Yes, sir. This is Stuat'ir. One hundred percent confidence."

As Nick watched, the shaky, trembling figure before him evaporated. The shoulders straightened, the eyes became dark and menacing, and an arrogant smile formed on the pale lips. Stuat'ir was a Xeyrian, a race of traders known for their ruthless approach to business. Xeyrian traders were rumored to have left a trail of vaporized bodies across the galaxy except this had never been proven since no living witnesses had ever been found after one of their trade deals went bad.

Nick often wondered how Stuat'ir ended up working with Gears as part of an engineering team on an Alliance Navy ship, but until now had never explored the question further. Then it didn't seem important because, as far as they knew until recently, Stuat'ir was killed when the *Heinlein* jumped to light speed.

Nick drew his blaster pistol from his holster and made a show of checking the charge to give this slimy piece of garbage more time to think. He pointed the weapon at the transformed trader, aiming between the eyes. "Stuat'ir," he growled between gritted teeth. "I'm going to ask you a lot of questions, but for right now all I want to know is who are you working for?"

Stuat'ir's eyes flitted to Bones, who glared at him, then shifted to Gears, who seemed equally unhappy to see him. He finally looked back at Nick, his eyes now uncertain. "If you kill me, you'll learn nothing," he said, his voice low.

Nick smirked. "Then I'll know nothing more than I know now. But I will have the satisfaction of knowing you're dead this time." He shook his head. "A lot of good people died because you provided Intel to that enemy fleet back in '27. A lot of them were friends of mine."

"You have no proof I had anything to do with that.." His voice trailed off as he looked from Bones to Gears until he stopped once again on Nick and the pistol staring him in the face. "I work for the Master," he blurted. "Please don't…"

Nick's lips formed a wry grin and he lowered the pistol. "Now that's a good start—"

"Captain," interrupted the SIN. "There is an incoming ship approaching at high speed. Its defensive screens have been raised and its weapons systems are armed and ready to fire."

"How far?" barked Nick.

"Five thousand kilometers approaching at point nine light speed."

"SIN," Nick said into the suit comm over an open channel. There was no more need for covert codes now. "Transport us and Stuat'ir back to the *Lightning*, then get us out of here," Nick said, holstering his pistol. "Bones, once we're aboard, secure Stuat'ir in a cabin. Gears and I will head for the flight deck."

Nick felt the familiar tingle associated with the transport beam and found himself standing in the materializer bay. "Sir, we have a greater problem," said the SIN. "It appears they have a weapons lock on us."

Gears shot a confused look at Nick.

Nick had to think of something fast. "Okay, SIN, put the alien space station between us and the incoming ship. We'll use it as shield until we come up with something better."

Gears shrugged.

By the time Nick and Gears erupted from the lift car, the flight deck beneath bucked and trembled, causing Nick's heart to skip a beat. "SIN, what's happening?" he asked as he dropped into the copilot's seat.

"The space station has been destroyed by the incoming vessel," replied the AI.

Gears was now seated in the pilot's seat, his fingers frantically touching the screen in front of him, working the ship control icons on the display. "We have temporarily maneuvered out of range of the attacking vessel. It has slowed but is coming about to take another pass. According to my scans, we will not survive a full blaster cannon burst."

Nick glared at Gears. "What do you mean? I thought this ship had defensive screens."

Gears shrugged while he worked the controls, sending them on a course to take them on a vector away from the incoming ship's flight path. "As I said, Captain, this ship is experimental. It's not a combat vessel."

"So we have no screens beyond navigation?" Gears didn't respond. Nick frantically considered their options until he landed on the one that had the most chance of success. "Gears, take us into Poseidon's oceans. If that alien fleet can survive in the ocean, why not us? It also might help us become a needle in that haystack we talked about earlier." Then it dawned on him. "And make sure you place us as close as possible to one of those ships so our attacker will have trouble determining which ship is which." He swallowed hard. *At least I hope so.*

"Strap in," Gears announced over the ship-wide comm. Nick secured his shoulder straps and clicked the buckle across the middle of his chest, connecting the two straps just before Gears tipped the *Lightning*'s nose over and started a steep dive into Poseidon's atmosphere. The forward-facing camera displayed on Nick's center screen showed the image of the planet coming at them rapidly, growing in size until the flames of reentry filled the screen and blocked his view of the planet.

Within a few seconds of reaching the lower atmosphere, the flames cleared and Nick saw the massive blue ocean far below; scattered white clouds whisked by as they rapidly descended.

Nick was being pressed hard against the chair back and his stomach seemed to be in his throat as the gravity compensator struggled to keep up with the speed the ship had achieved.

The ocean grew rapidly closer and closer and Nick began to worry they would hit it hard. Hitting water at high speed was like striking the ground, only the ground would be softer. The ship wouldn't survive the impact. "Uh, Gears, shouldn't we be slowing down?"

Glancing to his right, he saw Gears was in the zone. When in a state of deep concentration, the tech genius never responded to any external stimuli. And in Nick's experience, it was pointless to try. Nick squeezed his eyes shut and waited as the ship spiraled downward faster and faster. Suddenly his body became lighter and his broad shoulders pressed upward, hard against the seat straps.

He opened one eye to look at his tri-screens to discover they had slowed enough that they'd enter the ocean at a low enough speed to avoid breaking up. He breathed a sigh of relief.

"We're not out of the woods yet," said Gears grimly. He nodded at the sensor readings on his right screen, the same location as the readouts on Nick's screens.

Nick looked at the data on his screen and realized the enemy vessel was only a few minutes behind. They must have hesitated when they saw the *Lightning* disappear into the atmosphere and no doubt had to bleed off some speed before coming after them. Whoever was piloting that ship wanted them dead. *It must be the same ones who tried to kill us in the Sol system,* Nick thought sternly.

The *Lightning* speared the blue-green sea's surface and, once under the surface of the ocean, the ship's forward momentum began to slow further due to the increased drag created by the water. To compensate, Gears increased power to the thrusters and they soon sank deeper in the increasingly murky ocean. Visibility on Nick's screen was very quickly swallowed by inky darkness.

"Can't we engage the external navigation lights?" Nick suggested.

Gears shook his head. "Not a good idea. The enemy vessel has broken the surface about a kilometer from our position. The navigation lights would make us an easy target. I'm using the sensors to steer. We don't need to see where we're going to know where we're going." He shot a look of surprise at Nick.

"The trouble I've been having getting clear sensor readings disappeared once we broke the ocean's surface. Now I'm getting almost more data than our systems can handle."

Nick looked over; data streamed across Gears' three screens faster than his eyes could follow. His brow wrinkled. "How is that possible?" Gears shrugged and Nick decided to let it go for now. *One mystery at a time.*

"I'm picking up plasma drive readings about fifteen kilometers north of our position at a depth of approximately fifty kilometers," Gears said tersely. "And I'm picking up something I can't explain."

"What?" Nick's eyes scanned the data until he realized what he was seeing. The readings were of buildings on the ocean floor. Living buildings. A city comprised of living structures.

16

ESS Lightning
Ocean floor of Theta Pergonae IV aka Poseidon
4152.10.20 Galactic

It WAS AFTER midnight, ship's time, when they arrived over the massive fleet of heavily armed starships spread far and wide across the ocean floor. The fleet's running lights were lit, so they were able to see the ships closest to their position. The myriad green, white, and red lights trailed off in all directions until they were swallowed by the blackness. Like most planets in the galaxy, sunlight from the planet's star couldn't penetrate much more than two hundred meters into an ocean's depths.

"Have they detected us?" asked Bones from the weapons station.

Gears shook his head. He hadn't been able to keep the stealth shields engaged due to having to divert all power other than the thrusters and life support to their navigation shields and the hull integrity grid as they went deeper.

The increase in pressure on the hull at these depths would crush an unprotected starship as easily as if it were an eggshell.

Nick ignored the others while he studied the readings of the living cities. The buildings were made of organisms he had never encountered anywhere else in his travels. They were a hybrid between crustaceans, humanoids, and chondrichthyes—more commonly known in the Earth's ecosystem as sharks. Whether they were naturally occurring on this planet or, like his friends, transformed from something else remained a nagging question in the back of his mind. If they were capable of communicating with them was unknown.

"Any sign of that ship following us?" Nick said to no one in particular.

"No, sir," said Gears as he brought the ship to hover within ten meters of a large battlewagon at least a hundred times larger than the *Lightning*.

Nick's eyes flitted to his center screen that showed the image of a large warship. Glowing in the soft light from the ship's running lights was a massive tri-barreled blaster cannon, extending from the hull and set on a rotating platform. Nick arched an eyebrow upon seeing this vessel on the screen.

There had to be a least a thousand such ships hidden under this ocean. With this much firepower, someone planned to start a war.

It had to be the Master.

He spun his seat toward Gears. "Any signs we're being scanned by this fleet?"

"None that I can detect," Gears said.

Nick nodded as his stomach muscles tightened. "SIN, have you located Siren and the Kid's life signs?"

The Systems Information Network could operate the ship's sensors faster and with more detail than any human was capable, even Gears.

"Yes, Captain, they are fourteen meters from our current position."

They were in the ship just below them? How had this happened? It had to be more than a coincidence. He arched an eyebrow at Gears, who wore a weak grin on his pale features.

"I used their DNA as a beacon to determine our course. Can't let the AI make me look bad." He shrugged his narrow shoulders. "And besides, I had to use something as a navigation marker. I thought the DNA scans you made of Siren and the Kid at the space station might prove useful."

Nick smiled. "Good work, Gears." He turned in his chair to look at Bones. "We'll have to board that battlewagon. You game?" The big man's eyes narrowed and his mouth formed a grim line. Nick nodded and turned back to look at Gears.

"What went wrong with those stealth shields?"

Gears' ocular implants whirred in the quiet, mimicking a look of surprise. "You and Bones aren't planning to use them again after what happened."

Nick chuckled. "Yes, I am, but not for what you're thinking."

17

Unknown starship
Ocean floor of Theta Pergonae IV aka Poseidon
4152.10.20 Galactic

Bones AND Nick materialized on the alien
warship in their head-to-toe combat blast armor
with their blaster pistols at the ready in the empty
corridor. Nick also had his portable scanner at the
ready, gripped in his left hand. The small screen on
the unit displayed the coordinates of the room where
Siren and the Kid were being held. After checking the
readings on the scanner, he tilted his head at Bones,
indicating they should go to their right.

He hoped they didn't encounter any guards, at
least until they entered the room where their friends
were being held. The scanner tether attached to his
left wrist tugged at him when he started moving as
quickly and silently as possible along the corridor.
The lighting was subdued, possibly due to this being
nighttime on the starship or as a power conservation
measure.

The crushing pressure against the battlewagon's hull meant the vessel's hull integrity grid had to be drawing a lot of power. Nick wondered if they were using their internals sensors, but since they weren't using their external sensors, he doubted it. He spotted the security cameras, one at each end of the corridor, so their time without being discovered here was probably limited.

They hurried along the corridor, their sound-absorbing combat boots making their movements barely detectable. The exception was the sound of Caddowth's bare feet against deck plating that made a loud slapping noise with each step. Unfortunately there was no way to avoid the sound, but Nick didn't want their prisoner seen if they got into a firefight.

They quickly came to the door they were looking for. Nick shoved the scanner into the belt holster designed for the device and indicated Bones should move to the other side of the door. After the big man was in position, he pressed one gloved hand flat against the surface of the door and pressed hard, hoping it would open. It refused to move. He looked for a control pad but the walls were smooth and unmarred. He retrieved the scanner again and used it to determine where the locking mechanism for the door was located.

It appeared to be operated by a remote handheld device of a type he had never encountered before. The software schematics didn't make sense to his un-technical eye. Gears might able to make sense of this mess, but since they would be discovered sooner than later the longer they stayed here, he would have to make a decision now.

Nick frowned and reached for the implosion grenade on his belt. He looked at Bones, who understood immediately.

The big man backed away farther down the corridor, then pressed his back against the wall while looking away from the impending explosive flash before the door could collapse in on itself, crushed like a used tin can.

Nick had no idea exactly what a tin can was, but his grandfather said his great-granddad used to stomp on tin cans to flatten them when he was a boy. He couldn't picture it until he saw what an implosion grenade could do to structures and objects and even humanoids.

"Get behind me. And look away," he whispered before he activated the grenade, then pressed the magnetic strip on the side of the weapon against the stubborn door.

Nick then rushed to the opposite end of the corridor from Bones and turned his head away from the blast area. The grenade had a fifteen-second delay. He counted down in his head until two seconds before the implosion, when he heard Bones signal the door at his end of the corridor had opened. It was too late to stop the grenade from going off.

He felt the pull of the implosion before he heard any sound. Implosion grenades not only compressed matter in on itself but also muffled most of the sound of the violent reaction. What he did hear quite loudly was screams of extreme pain.

Nick's heart beat faster and he worried if those screams came from Bones or his prisoner. After waiting ten seconds, he stole a look at the site of the explosion and beyond, and saw Bones kneeling over a body lying face down on the deck.

Nick moved to check on the door, and the grenade had indeed made it collapse on itself. It lay in a smoking wreck, crumpled like tissue paper on the deck. He peered into the room, which was shrouded in darkness.

He activated the night vision feature in the visor of his helmet and the room's interior became visible in the soft green light's sweeping arc.

The two containment tanks stood in the middle of the room but they appeared inactive. On the floor lay three bodies: two were obviously guards dressed in odd looking uniforms though of military design, the third was a large, four-armed Lobsan female wearing the traditional sleeveless burnt orange shirt and baggy gray pants common on her home world. This meant she was a civilian, something Nick hadn't expected to find on these military starships.

He looked down the corridor to see Bones had disarmed the injured alien guard, its weapon slung over his back—the weapon looked very much like an Alliance Navy issue blaster rifle—and was now carrying its limp form cradled in his muscular arms as if it were a child.

When they met at the entrance to the darkened room, he saw the shape of the guard meant it was female; the face was, however, obscured by the opaque faceplate of the helmet that covered the head. Nick nodded at Bones, then slipped inside the smoky room with the large man right behind him carrying the limp guard.

They moved quickly across the room, accompanied by the sound of coughing. "Okay," Nick whispered to his unseen charge.

"Deactivate the stealth shield and get dressed in one these guard's uniforms." Nick nodded to one empty corner and pointed to Bones to indicate he should set his prisoner there. Then Bones helped Nick drag the other three unconscious humanoids to the corner and sat them beside each other. Thankfully they were still breathing.

A naked, shivering, coughing Caddowth shimmered into view. Her purple skin was covered in goose bumps due to the cooler air in the room. Nick had no empathy at all for this traitor. She would have sacrificed their lives if need be and he wasn't about to allow himself to feel anything but contempt for her. The problem was, they needed her to find some way to reverse the transformation of Siren and the Kid.

"It's about time," she said, her voice trembling. She moved to stand over the unconscious guards and looked them over, arching one eyebrow when her gaze stopped on the female. "I hope she's wearing undergarments."

Bones knelt next to the female guard and unlatched the helmet first. He pulled it off and froze. "Boss…"

Nick had turned his attention to the two containment tanks, looking for some controls to restart them so he could see if his friends were inside. He had found a small control pad covered in a symbolic-based language he had never seen before—and he had seen a lot of alien symbol-based languages in his travels. He made sure to record the characters with his handheld scanner to show them to Gears and the SIN later. Between them they might be able to make some sense of the symbols.

"Sir," Bones said more forcefully. "You *really* need to see this…"

Nick grunted, annoyed at the interruption. "What is it?" He turned to see what Bones was so determined he must see immediately. He froze and nearly dropped the scanner. "Sonara?" he whispered.

18

NICK HAD CHANGED into his flight suit jumper as soon as they returned to the *Lightning*. He stood with his arms crossed over his chest, one eyebrow arched on his scarred forehead, looking at the two containment tanks still smelling of salty seawater resting on the deck of the materializer bay. They had brought the tanks aboard along with Siren's unconscious sister, Sonara, and a fully clothed Caddowth, without being detected.

A stealth shield had hidden her presence. If the security footage in the corridor was reviewed, all anyone would see would be two armed beings in battle armor, their faces obscured by helmets. Any security cameras in what turned out to be a research lab had been knocked out when the implosion bomb went off and cut the power to the room.

Nick didn't want anyone to make the connection between Caddowth and Blaster Squad. At least, not yet.

Nick's heart beat faster than normal as anxiety rose from his belly. He sorely wanted to begin pacing but he held himself in check. Gears was busy adapting cable interfaces from the ship's internal energy grid to provide power to the two tanks. Nick had already confirmed the transformed Siren and the Kid were inside the tanks but they appeared to be struggling to breathe. The SIN's scans confirmed the oxygen content of the water was steadily dropping. Time was running short.

Finally Gears finished and managed to power up the two tanks. A soft green glow was now visible through the observation windows of both tanks, and the control panels lit up. The symbols glowed bright yellow against the gray burnished steel pads.

Nick moved to the closest control panel, his fingers hovering over the pad. He was uncertain if he should touch anything. Common sense told him he shouldn't but he was frustrated by his helplessness at reading these alien symbols. "Gears, what should we do?"

"SIN," said Gears. "Scan the tank's interior. What's the water temperature?"

"Thirty-five degrees Celsius," replied the AI.

"Life and oxygen readings?"

"Stable. The oxygen level is returning to optimal."

Gears sighed and looked at Nick. His face was gray and worn due to a lack of sleep. "It appears they are going to be okay for now, but we have to find a way to change them back to fully human. According to SIN's bio-scans, they have been changed into a hybrid. I have no idea how to reverse the process." He snorted in frustration. "In fact, I have no idea how they did this in the first place."

Nick held up the sealed, clear glass vial he had found when he searched Sonara before Bones locked her up in a cabin with Caddowth, who protested all the while. The cabin was tight for one person, never mind two grown women.

"What do our scans tell us about the contents of this vial?"

The SIN responded. "The vial contains a suspension fluid denser than water. Suspended within the liquid are trillions of organic nano-bots—"

Gears interrupted the AI's explanation. "— We don't know what they do or how they were manufactured, but as far as we can determine, they are living machines." He crossed his arms and his brow creased.

"They might be connected to the transformation process or they might not be, we have no way of knowing." He shook his head. "We're flying in the dark here, Captain."

Nick scowled at the tech genius and considered his and the SIN's information, then quickly came to a decision. "Wake up Sonara and bring her here." Bones opened his mouth to speak but Nick silenced him with a steely glare. Siren's deceitful sister had been carrying the vial, so she might have answers to their questions. He just had to be on his guard with her. She couldn't be trusted.

Fifteen minutes passed, which gave Nick and Gears the opportunity to look over the controls and the latches and hinges of the two tanks. If they discovered a way to open the tank, they would need to know more about it. SIN warned if the water in the tank drained out, the beings inside would very quickly be unable to breath unless they were immediately re-submersed in water or they were transformed to air breathers.

Nick concluded any attempt to open the tanks was risky to his friends' survival unless they had made adequate preparations. That was where Sonara came in.

The lift doors opened and Bones pushed Siren's sister out of the car ahead of him. Her hair, usually long and shiny, was now only a trace of black stubble that covered her pale scalp. Her dead eyes looked at him, the spark of life absent behind those brilliant blue orbs. She appeared to be a beaten woman, with her shoulders hunched forward making her appear far older than he knew she was. It was also the first time he noticed that her suit armor was scarred and dented, her cheeks sunken, and she appeared gaunt as if she hadn't eaten in a few days or even a week or two. His nose wrinkled slightly. And the smell coming from her indicated she hadn't showered in a while as well.

Not that he cared but she must have been put through hell by whoever was behind this fleet.

"Sonara," Nick said, his tone deep and threatening. "I need to know how to change your sister back."

Sonara gazed at him in silence for several seconds, then she said, "Do you have the vial?" Nick nodded and held it out for her to see. "Good. Then after we deploy the nano-bots, it will take about forty-eight hours for her to revert to human."

"Hold on," protested Gears, stepping forward.

"We don't know how these nano-bots work or where they come from or if what you say is true. I have never seen as much as a scientific paper anywhere in the Alliance about such technology."

Sonara emitted a weary sigh. "I know you don't trust me. I get it. But I was on my way to deploy the nano-bots myself to save my sister when Bones stopped me." Her eyes flitted to the muscular half Martian, then back to Nick. "She and the Kid were used as guinea pigs to test the technology. Once it proves successful, they plan to transform the millions of the inhabitants of this planet."

Nick's eyes narrowed. "For what purpose?"

Sonara sighed again. "To build an army." She locked eyes with him, the corners of her own drooping. "To mount an invasion and assume control of the galaxy."

19

IT HAD BEEN four days since leaving Poseidon and Nick had watched Sonara eat everything that wasn't nailed down. Nailed down was an odd expression, but he still had to remind himself to keep his hands away from the edges of each plate of food he placed before their talkative prisoner or he'd lose an appendage. They had managed to evade any enemy patrols and so far it appeared no enemy vessels had followed them.

Sonara sat across the galley table from him, working her way through a lunch of spaghetti and meatballs, her angular chin splashed with streaks of rich red tomato sauce.

Gears and Bones sat with them on the remaining sides of the four-seat table, eating their ham and cheese sandwiches, listening to the conversation, Bones offering his captain the occasional humorless grin.

They both looked very uncomfortable having this traitor aboard ship.

Nick was impressed by the variety of cuisine the food synthesizer aboard the *Lightning* provided them. The choice of meals was far more than the *Hunter*'s synthesizer was capable of producing.

He spooned the last bit of lime gelatin into his mouth, the sweet-sour taste bright against his taste buds as he watched Sonara eating like someone possessed. She had taken a long shower before changing into a plain gray-brown jumpsuit, and the color in her cheeks had improved in direct proportion to the rest and good food she'd had in the past few days.

Before leaving Poseidon, she administered an equal portion of the nano-bots to Siren and the Kid, explaining the vial contained enough of the microscopic living machines to help them both recover. She divided the contents of the vial into two quantities since she said the vial only contained one dose for one person, explaining it would take four days at a minimum rather than two to complete the transformation due to the lower concentration of nano-bots.

Nick wondered why she didn't have a second vial or if she had only intended to save her sister?

He decided to let it go for now since she readily agreed to divide the nano-bots between his two friends. So far he hadn't detected any deception in her manner or words, but his deep-seated suspicion of her remained.

Gears rigged an atmosphere exchanger to the two containment tanks to link them with the *Lightning*'s life support systems, so as Siren and the Kid changed back to air breathers, the water in the tank would gradually be replaced by an oxygen/nitrogen atmosphere. SIN would monitor the transformation and make any needed adjustments to the environment within the tanks as the process proceeded. Nick had never been as thankful as he was today to have a System Information Network artificial intelligence incorporated into every Alliance starship. He vowed never to let anyone disparage the usefulness of a SIN again.

"So tell me more about the Master and the structure of his forces," Nick said before raising his coffee cup to his lips and taking a sip.

Sonara slurped in the last of the noodles hanging from her between her lips, then swallowed before responding.

"I've been undercover for the past five months but they didn't provide me with an organizational chart. However, I can tell you an Imperial Legate named Kopeck is in charge of the fleet you discovered on the sea bed of Poseidon's ocean."

Nick, Gears, and Bones exchanged knowing glances. "Do you mean Alliance Council board member Anton Kopeck?" Nick asked, his stomach muscles tightening. When Gears had discovered their other passenger with Kopeck, it had triggered this entire mission. Stuat'ir, transformed to appear as a human scientist, remained locked in a cabin, as did Commander Caddowth. Nick had begun to think of the *Lightning* more as a prison ship than a prototype FTL vessel. The real problem was they didn't carry enough operational FTL stasis pods for them and their prisoners.

Sonara didn't appear to notice the exchange of looks since her eyes still locked on the remaining half a meatball and dwindling supply of spaghetti on her plate. "Yes, I believe so," she said after swallowing another forkful of spaghetti.

Nick reached across the table to grab Sonara's wrist just before she stabbed the half meatball. She looked up into his eyes. He saw the old deceitful Sonara behind those brilliant azure eyes.

Coupled with a trace of arrogance, it made Nick's anger increase exponentially. "I think you're lying," he growled between gritted teeth.

Sonara's dark eyebrows rose simultaneously. "Really, Nick? What reason would I have to lie?"

Bones jumped into the discussion. "You are trying to save your own skin. You know we're short one FTL stasis pod." He snorted derisively. "You'd say anything, even this fantasy about Kopeck and some…" His voice trailed off his cheeks flushing a deep red. He threw the half of his uneaten sandwich onto the plate in front of him, rose to his feet, and stomped toward the lift, soon disappearing behind the lift doors.

Nick's eyes narrowed. "He might be right, of course." He paused. "At least that's one explanation. I prefer to think you and I have mutual self-interest."

"And what would that be, Captain?" she said, her voice deeper and more threatening.

"You aren't Sonara," he said after a brief pause. "This decrepit look of yours is all an act. You're one of the aliens transformed to appear human hoping at some point you'd be captured and be delivered to the heart of the Alliance." Nick offered her a wry grin. "But someone didn't expect Blaster Squad would find you since we know the real Sonara so well."

He paused. "Why did you have the vial to cure Siren with you?"

The transformed alien glared at him. "We were going to use it as an inducement to make her talk by promising her a cure. It would have worked too if you hadn't interfered."

Nick cleared his throat. These aliens didn't know Siren very well. She would never have given up any information even if it meant her death. "Now you're going to tell me what I need to know about you and your race and why you've aligned with the Master." He was fishing about these aliens falling in with the Master but the look of arrogance in her eyes told him all he needed to know.

The pseudo Sonara chuckled humorlessly. "I don't think I'm going to tell you anything more." She stood. Gears stood as well. He had a blaster pistol pointed at her. "I had hoped my deception would remain undetected until we reached your system of origin. We need to know more about your defenses and your weaknesses. We already know a great deal about your physiology, but we need more information to complete our profile of the Alliance." Her eyes narrowed, following Nick as he rose to his feet.

"So you can defeat us in battle?" Nick said. She didn't respond but he could see her answer in her eyes.

"SIN, signal Bones to bring Caddowth here." He offered a tight-lipped smile to Sonara. "And tell him not be *too* rough with her." Just as he expected, a hint of concern flashed across the alien's eyes.

Bones soon arrived, grasping Caddowth by her left arm. She avoided Nick's gaze, but her eyes widened slightly when she saw Sonara. Nick had moved across the room and now stood with his arms crossed, observing the interaction between the two alien females.

"Bones, aim your blaster pistol at Caddowth and prepare to fire. Make sure it's set to kill." Bones glanced at him, then pulled his pistol from the holster on his belt and stepped back after releasing her arm. He checked the weapon's setting, then took aim at Caddowth's head.

Nick regarded Sonara sternly. "You have ten seconds to start telling me what I want to know." He dropped his arms to his sides. "The truth this time."

Sonara and Caddowth exchanged a look. Caddowth nodded to her, telling Nick part of what he needed to know.

"All right, Captain, I will tell you everything. Just please do not kill Consort Caddowth."

Nick arched one eyebrow. "Consort Caddowth. Consort to who?"

"The Emperor," said Sonara, her features hardening.

20

ESS Lightning
Nearing Earth system Defense Grid
4152.11.2 Galactic

THE SHIP HAD been dropped from FTL travel the day before and they had been traveling at .99 light speed for the past twenty-four hours. Gears had modified the materializer to *borrow* sufficient plasma fuel from the enemy battlewagon to power their FTL engine. By the time the battlewagon crew discovered the missing fuel, the *Lightning* would be long gone.

Nick had signaled their security code to the closest Defense Grid outpost as they came within communications range. With the loss of Pluto Station, the Navy had redeployed the remaining outposts to maintain equal coverage across the grid, or as close to equal as possible. Hopefully repairs to the station would be complete in the next few months.

Nick had instructed the SIN to drop out of FTL flight mode farther out than normal so he would have time to decide what they would tell Chairman Whizzar.

Gears had converted the containment tanks to adapt them as FTL stasis pods for Siren and the Kid. Thankfully they had worked perfectly and Siren and the Kid had awoken fully human and in perfect physical health.

They didn't recall a lot about what had happened to them. Siren said the experience was more like a terrible dream. Nick worried they would suffer long-term effects, but for now they seemed fine. Once they reached Earth, he'd suggest they seek out examination and treatment to determine any issues that may arise later, especially those beyond the physical.

The mission had been a success as far as it went, but now he had to decide what to do with Caddowth and the duplicate of Sonara. Neither, it seemed, was who they originally claimed to be and both owed allegiance to this Master, who it seemed had ambitions to overthrow the Alliance and rule the galaxy as Emperor, modeled after the ancient Roman Empire. And this Master was transforming millions of beings of an ancient alien race, and possibly others, to use as soldiers to amass an army to operate the largest fleet of heavily armed starships ever assembled.

At present this fleet had begun to assemble on Poseidon, so they were at least three months from the Earth system if they left today.

However, the fake Sonara told them it would take at least eight months to transform the inhabitants of Kodrus—this is the aliens' name for their world, code named Poseidon by the Alliance. For now the fleet was gathering, but possibly what they'd detected was only part of a larger fleet the Master was massing.

The fake Sonara had been very angry when she discovered Nick's threat to kill Caddowth had been a ruse to get her to talk and that, with Gears jury-rigging the containment tanks, they had enough FTL pods for everyone. He smiled at the memory of her face becoming a dark shade of red and her body trembling with fury. *Some days are just better than others*, he mused. Of course Caddowth was not very happy with him either since he had made her use a stealth shield to board the enemy battlewagon so she had to transport without clothing. When she asked him why, his reply was, "A pile-on of humiliation."

Right now Gears sat beside Nick in the pilot's seat on the flight deck of the *Lightning*. Bones sat at the weapons station, the Kid at communications, and Siren at sensors and monitoring ship systems. The SIN could take over the ship in an emergency but Nick had always been more comfortable with a humanoid crew in charge of his starship.

It might be called a prejudice against technology, but he had grown up surrounded by technology so he knew his feelings went far deeper than this simplistic answer.

His views might have been formed during all the time he'd spent as a child with his grandfathers and the homespun wisdom the two men shared with him. Whatever created this need for human control over technology—instead of letting machines control everything—over time he had grown increasingly comfortable with his stand on technology and wasn't about to change any time soon.

"What do you plan to tell the chairman?" asked Gears without looking in his direction.

Nick sighed. "Let's just say I wish I had several weeks to decide. Unfortunately, I have an hour at most." He looked at the screen on the left side of his tri-screen array in the copilot's station. It showed the chairman was an hour away when they received the signal. The chairman had been making an onsite inspection of the Defense Grid when the *Lightning* signaled their impending arrival. Nick wondered if the timing of the chairman's sudden appearance was more than a coincidence.

The signal flashed to announce the arrival of the ANSS *Rosa Parks* not three thousand meters from their position. The Navy vessel quickly matched speed and course with them.

"Captain, the *Rosa Parks* signals they are ready to transport Chairman Whizzar aboard," said the Kid, sounding like he had never left his post, making Nick swallow a smile.

"Tell them I'll meet the chairman in the materializer bay in five minutes," Nick said as he rose from the copilot's seat. He stopped and scanned the faces of his crew, not lingering too long on any one face.

"First I want to say I am so grateful and pleased to have us all together again. I have missed flying with you." His words caught in his throat. He coughed, then narrowed his eyes at first Gears, then Siren, Bones, and lastly the Kid. "I'm meeting the chairman in my quarters. It's a *private* meeting. And I mean private. Any of you attempting to clandestinely monitor our discussions will find themselves walking home. Understood?"

He watched his crew offer reluctant nods, each in turn. "That goes for you as well, SIN. No audio or video recording of my meeting with the chairman. Understood?"

"Yes, Captain," replied the SIN. Nick thought he detected reluctance in the machine voice as well, but dismissed the idea. Machines don't have feelings, even those with advanced artificial intelligence. He stepped into the lift car and avoided looking at his loyal friends until they disappeared behind the lift doors.

The lift doors opened to reveal a six-foot-seven Edgar Whizzar, chairman of the Alliance Council and president and CEO of Terraform Incorporated, the largest planet transformation provider in the galaxy, who greeted him with a wide grin. He was dressed in a shiny black suit and powder-blue dress shirt. His curly black hair was longer than he normally wore it, meaning the chairman was under considerable stress not taking time out for a haircut. His intense hazel eyes were wrinkled at the corners and he seemed genuinely pleased to see Nick.

His right hand came out as Nick stepped onto the deck. "Nick, so nice to see you again. Congratulations on the rescue of Siren and Alfonso Ripe, who I think you and your crew call the Kid if I'm not mistaken."

Nick offered a tight smile. Nick then took the man's warm, fleshy hand into his and shook it firmly. "Nice to see you as well, Chairman."

"Now, now, Nick, let's not stand on formalities. Call me Edgar. I insist," he added after seeing the hesitation in Nick's eyes.

Am I really that transparent? "Let's talk in my cabin," Nick said, turning toward the lift doors.

The chairman stepped up beside him but didn't look in his direction. Neither Nick nor the chairman spoke after they boarded the lift or as they walked along the corridor to his quarters. It wasn't until the door to his quarters closed that the chairman whirled to face him.

The jovial, pleasant, grinning Edgar Whizzar had disappeared, replaced by a weary man feeling the tremendous pressure of his office. "Are we being monitored?" he asked grimly.

"No, sir," Nick said. "I ordered my crew and the SIN to keep this conversation off the record."

Whizzar nodded as he took a seat at Nick's desk. Nick leaned against the side of his bed. "Good." He crossed his arms over his wide chest and regarded Nick with one eyebrow raised. "Tell me about this Master."

Nick began at the beginning when they had been attacked by the *Mars Explorer* just outside the Earth system, then the subsequent attack of Pluto Station by unknown vessels.

He then told the chairman about the massive fleet on Kodrus, the deception by Caddowth and the double for Sonara. Lastly he outlined the threat to the Alliance posed by the nano-bots that transformed living beings, the build-up of an army of transformed soldiers, and the amassing of the massive fleet for the Master, who the altered Sonara said had Imperial ambitions.

The chairman's brow wrinkled. "A would-be Emperor, is it?" He dropped his arms to his sides. "We have a lot of work ahead of us." He gazed into Nick's eyes. "Will you help?"

Nick didn't want to be more involved than he was already, but he knew the future of Blaster Squad and the galaxy was too large a stake not to take sides. "Yes, Chairman, my crew and I stand ready to defend the Alliance."

The chairman's eyes narrowed. "Who can we trust?"

"Truthfully? No one. But we have to trust someone if we're going to save the Alliance." Nick withheld the information about Anton Kopeck's meet up with the not-so-dead Stuat'ir because he might need a hole card later.

The chairman nodded, then looked away to the wall with the picture of a Telus II geyser spewing a stream of scalding water high into the air. "We'll have to persuade your prisoners to provide more information. Don't you think?"

Nick grunted, then nodded grimly. It looked like Blaster Squad was headed into territory where they had never been before.

Blaster Squad will return in *Galaxy of Evil*.

About the Author

International selling Star Trek author, Russ Crossley, writes science fiction and fantasy, and mystery/suspense as well as their various subgenres.

His latest science fiction satire set in the far future, Revenge of the Lushites, is a sequel to Attack of the Lushites released in 2011. Both titles are available in e-book and trade paperback.

He has sold several short stories that have appeared in anthologies from various publishers including; WMG Publishing, Pocket Books, 53rd Street Publishing, and St. Martins Press.

He is a member of SF Canada and is past president of the Greater Vancouver Chapter of Romance Writers of America. He is also an alumni of the Oregon Coast Professional Fiction Writers Master Class taught by award winning author/editors, Kristine Katherine Rusch and Dean Wesley Smith.

Feel free to contact him on Facebook, Twitter, or his website http//:www.russcrossley.com. He loves to hear from readers.

Other titles by Russ Crossley you may enjoy

Razor and Edge Mysteries
The Kidnapping of Billy Buttons
String of Pearls
Death by Clown
Beggin' For Murder
Ragged Ice
The Grand Central Mystery
A Strange Case of Undead Murder

Jazz Stiletto Mysteries
A Day Without Sunshine
Skullduggery
Instrument of justice (first published in Over My
Dead Body online mystery magazine)

The Amanda Dark paranormal mysteries
Hook Island
Grind Manor
Moonrise Diner
A Father's Daughter

The Trudy Wilson Mystery Novel Series
Bad Loyalty
Shear Murder
Buzzcut - coming soon

Blaster Squad
#1 Terror on the Moon

#2 Sea of Death
#3 Planet of Doom
#4 Raiders of Cloud City
#5 Rise of the Empire

Other Novels

Attack of the Lushites
Revenge of the Lushites
My Zombie Prince
Antique Virgin
The Fire In Their Hearts
with R.S. Meger (from Champagne Books)
Zomopolis
The Last Serial Killer

Short Stories
Countdown
Shoeless Moe
Round Up At The Burger Bar:
The Story of Trixie Pug, Parts 1, 2, 3, 4, 5, 6, 7, 8, 9
Five Minutes
Blossom Queen, Barbarian
The Secret
The Family Line
End of the Flies
Death by Magic
The Penguin Sleeps With The Fishes
Only The Worthy
Hero For A Day
End of Empire
Strange Bedfellows

Big Business
A Perfect Crime
The Wise Guy and The Pirates
In Search of the Perfect Cup
T.I.N. Men
The Legend of G and the Dragonettes
The Incredible Mr. Fix-It
Lock Stock and Barrel
Divided Loyalties
Cave of Wonders
A Family Empire
Until We Meet Again
Dragon Rising
Solitary Man
The Keel Mountain Conspiracy
Angel on My Shoulder
Heroes of Old
The Great Bicycle Race
Tikka's Big Day
"My Partner the Zombie" —
Hungry For Your Love Anthology
(St. Martin's Press)
Big Hairy Deal
One Red Shoe
A Bad Day in Lunden Texas
Bloody Betty, Queen of the Pirates
Mirror Image
Dangerous Waters
Cape Disappointment
Boomerang
The Watcher of Wayburn Street
The Apprentice

Drip!
A Beautiful Friendship and The Parrot of Doom
Robine's Diary
The Christmas Club
Loose Ends
Splatter Pattern
It Takes Two
Lexicon
Replacement Parts
Sidekicks
Lost Stories
Time and Space
Survivors
Neighborhood Watch
Unnatural Immortal
Rum Runner's Lounge
It's A Small Galaxy
A Shattered Man
Betrayed
Replacement Parts
Clubhouse Heroes
Sounds That Angels Make
Muggins Rules – originally published in Fiction River
Volume 12, Risk Takers

Anthologies
Tales of Urban Fantasy
Five Tales of Bizarre Detectives
Tales of Mystery and Suspense
Tales of Weird Fantasy
Tales of Twisted Crime
Tales of The Unexpected

Tales From Space
10 by Russ Crossley
Round Up At The Burger Bar: The Story of Trixie Pug,
Parts 1- 5 The Beginning
Worlds of Science Fiction and Fantasy
More Tales of Mystery and Suspense
Justice Served
Love Stories
Ladies of the Jolly Roger with Rita Schulz
The Adventures of Razor and Edge:
Five Tales From The Quirky Detective Team
An Unexpected Journey
On Edge
Thrilling Adventures
Total War
Courageous

Non-Fiction
The Writers Tools - The Synopsis

Also available from 53rd Street Publishing

In this fourth Blaster Squad mission in the 42nd century a horrifying civil war rages when it's discovered someone is supplying the primitive world Feros III with advanced weapons.

Nick Justice and his intrepid mercenary squad Gears, Bones, Siren and the Kid are assigned to a covert mission to discover who is behind the supply of the powerful, death dealing weapons.

Blaster Squad infiltrates the planet only to discover a mysterious figure known only as the Master is behind not only the weapons, but also the threat extends to the stability of the galaxy itself.

In a race against time, with billions of lives are at stake, Nick and Blaster Squad must disrupt the Master's plans before all is lost.

These fast paced high stakes adventures continue so join with Blaster Squad in this tale of adventure and pulse pounding action to save the galaxy for all human and alien kind.